Quests of the Undead

My Life Among the Undead:

Book 9

Camara M. Bragdon

My Life among the Undead Books

By

Camara M. Bragdon

Friend of the Undead

Yard Sale of the Undead

Secrets of the Undead

Carnival of the Undead

Holiday of the Undead

Reunion of the Undead

Election of the Undead

Legacy of the Undead

DEDICATION

This book is dedicated to my awesome cat, my little buddy, Mister Mistoffelees.

CHAPTERS

Chapter One:
Moving Day

Moving can be pretty stressful. You've got packing boxes filled with stuff you didn't even know you had. Sometimes you have to move because your slimy landlord has decided to evict you for no good reason. Sometimes you have to move because you've decided to make a major career change from a librarian who can make telepathic communion with the undead to a telepathic vampire queen of a hidden chain of islands.

My husband, Eddie Van Helsing, lugged a box of our belongings into the main hallway of the Castle DeLorean. "That's the last one," my vampire said with a thankful sigh. Once he set the box down, he ran his fingers through his short, curly, jet-black hair.

I took one look around the colossal hallway, littered with boxes and furniture. "It's not so bad." I placed my hands on my hips. "At least, we'll have some help once we picked out our room. Gunther said we can have any one of the suites on the royal floor."

"I did see one with a balcony overlooking the garden."

I looked over at my husband. His five-foot, nine-inch, muscular frame fit nicely into his blue jeans and black and red AC/DC T-shirt. Every day, he got more and sexier. I smiled at him.

"What?" he asked.

"Just thinking about how much I love you," I replied.

He tucked a lock of my brown hair behind one of my ears. "Me too, Shelly. Or should I say, your Majesty?"

I shot a fanged grin at him. "Well, I'm not the queen yet."

"Your Highness," said a voice behind us.

We turned around to see a dignified, aging centaur wearing a white collared shirt under a gray vest standing before us. He got down on his forelegs to give me a deep bow. "I am Rupert Chincoteague, head butler here at Delorean Castle, at your Highness' service." He had a full head of gray hair

"Good to meet you, Rupert," I said. "This is my husband,

Eddie."

"Pleased to meet you, sir."

"Likewise," Eddie's unusual response received a surprised look from me.

Where did that come from? I asked him subliminally. As a vampire, I have many rare abilities; one is telepathic communication with the undead. The only undead person I do almost all of my mental contact with Eddie.

Since my wife is a queen, I might as well act dignified, he replied.

I turned back to Rupert. "Well, Rupert, could you show my husband and me to the royal private quarters?"

"Of course, your Highness," the half-man, half-horse said. He beckoned us to follow him to an elevator at the end of the hallway. He pressed the "up" button. "Have you been on a tour of the castle?"

"Yes, before we went back to Zephyr," Eddie said.

The elevator doors dinged open, and we stepped inside. "The royal quarters are beautiful. There are five large suites, each with a master bath and a private balcony," Rupert explained.

"How big are the balconies?"

"About ten by six," Rupert replied. "You can easily fit a swing and a grill on the balcony."

Eddie and I looked at each other as we liked the sound of that. On the fifth floor, we got off and followed our new butler to the suite at the back of the building. I flung open the cherry wood doors with tiny intricate floral designs and gasped in amazement. The suite was twice as large as your regular one-bedroom apartment. There was a full kitchen off to the left of the massive living room with a private balcony. On the right was the bedroom door, which Eddie flung open.

"I like the fireplace," I said, following him into the huge bedroom with the cathedral ceilings complete with skylights. The lush, velvet carpet felt good under my feet. I looked back at Rupert, who patiently stood in the suite's doorway. "I think we've got a winner."

"Good, I'll inform the servants to move your items. I believe Mr. Hornicus would like to meet you in the State Room to discuss your coronation."

"Sure," I said with a yawn. I glanced at my watch. It was getting late.

We climbed back on the elevator, and Eddie and I got off at the main floor and headed to the massive, fluorescent pink State Room. That was definitely going to be repainted. Sitting on an L-shaped black pleather couch was my new Private Secretary, Gunther Hornicus.

The fiftyish-year-old satyr wore a navy, three-piece suit. Two curved horns sat atop his balding head. He uncrossed his goat shaped legs before getting up to greet us. "Good evening, your Highness," he said.

"Good evening, Gunther," I said.

"Good evening, Sir Eddie," the satyr said with a nod. He turned to me, "Your Highness, I would like to discuss tomorrow's coronation with you."

I sat down on the couch opposite Gunther. "Go ahead," I said, trying to keep a yawn from escaping. I really began wishing that last bottle of fruit dragon blood I drank on the seven-hour flight over had caffeine in it. Stupid jet lag. I had only been a vampire for just over a month. I still couldn't find any bottled blood with caffeine. Those homemade, extra sugary doughnuts Leo made on the Monte Carlo were yummy and gave Eddie and me some extra energy, but now we were crashing.

"The coronation will take place at noon tomorrow, but Doctor Orlok has requested you meet with him in the Great Hall of the Melbourne Building at six for practice."

I winced at the thought of getting up that early. "Why?"

"Doctor Orlok believes practice makes perfect," the satyr replied with a hint of annoyance.

"Just how long is the coronation?" Eddie asked.

"It'll be a little over two hours," Gunther replied. "There will be speeches and singing. The queen will publicly appoint her new Guardian. After the coronation, you will also meet the members of Parliament at a very lavish luncheon in the Chaps and Spurs Casino."

"How many members of Parliament are there?" I asked.

"Well, about 50 of the islands are uninhabited. Therefore, there are only 50 members. Hopefully, the prime minister will give you more details after the coronation."

Eddie leaned forward in his seat. "What will my role be?"

"Well, you are her Guardian."

"But, I'm also married to her."

"Eddie would be a king consort, right?" I asked.

"Yes," Gunther said.

I tried to stifle another yawn.

The satyr gave me an apologetic look. "I'm sorry, your Highness. I'm keeping you up late." He reached into a pocket on the inside of his vest and pulled out several folded pieces of lined paper. "Doctor Orlok wants you to go over your speech."

"Speech?"

He handed me the papers. "This one."

I took it from him. "Thank you, Gunther. You can go."

My private secretary got up from his seat and gave me a deep bow. "Goodnight, your Highness," he said before leaving the State Room.

"Goodnight, Gunther," I said.

Eddie got up and pulled me off the couch. "Let's go to bed."

I glanced at the folded speech in my hands. "Geesh, this is five pages long! How does Doctor Orlok expect me to memorize this by noon?"

"He certainly has incredibly high hopes." We walked to the elevator, and Eddie pressed the button leading up to our suite. "So, what does the speech say?"

I started to skim it. "Eh, mostly flowery, superfluous crap. ' I promise to rule and regulate to the best of my abilities, according to the laws and morals of Peregrin.'"

"Regulate? Are you supposed to be the queen or the moral police?" The elevator dinged open, and we stepped inside. Eddie hit the fifth-floor button with his thumb.

"Listen to this line. ' I will make sure everyone is safe by establishing morality in every aspect of life.'" I crumbled up the papers. "Okay, if Doctor Orlok wants me to give a speech, I will give my own speech."

We got off the elevator and walked to our new suite. A young vampire and werewolf had finished delivering the last of our boxes and were about to open them. "Whoa!" I said. Rupert stepped into view. "Your Highness, Paul and Rueben were about to start unpacking, if that's alright with you."

"Don't worry about it. Eddie and I will handle it."

"Are you sure? We are at your disposal."

"It's fine. Go home and get some rest."

A look of surprise crossed the centaur's face. "Thank you, Your Highness. We'll be back here at nine in the morning." He motioned for the two servants to leave.

Eddie watched them get on the elevator and then looked at the piles of boxes and furniture strewn about the suite. He went into our bedroom. "You should've, at least, let them put our bed together."

I went in to see what he was talking about. Our cherry headboard, footboard, and box spring were leaning up against the wall in the massive room. The only other thing in the room was our bare mattress. I went back to the main suite and looked around for the bedding box. After a quick look, I found it on the top of pile number five. Peeling off the cover, I yanked out a teal blue fitted sheet, two pillows, and our floral comforter and carried everything into our new bedroom.

Eddie had already unpacked my red, satin nightgown and his navy blue and white plaid drawstring pants. "Need help with the bedding?" he asked.

"Yeah," I replied. Together we placed the sheet on the mattress and tossed the pillows on top along with the comforter. We'd set-up the bed tomorrow. Then we changed and crawled into bed. The castle was eerily quiet. "I thought the castle had guards on twenty-four hours."

"The sphinxes were given the night off due to our arrival," Eddie replied between yawns. He gave me a kiss. "Goodnight, babe."

"Goodnight, darling," I replied before drifting off to deep sleep.

Chapter Two:
Vincent Price Isn't Dead;
He's Peregrin's Minister of Virtue

A loud knocking on the door to our suite jarred us awake.

"What in the world?" Eddie asked as he propped himself up on both elbows. He glanced at his cell phone on the floor next to the mattress. "It's almost seven! Who is at the door at this hour?"

"Your Highness, it's almost time for your practice coronation," Gunther's hesitant voice echoed loudly on the other side of the door.

I literally jumped out of bed. "Oh, crap, I totally forgot!" I threw on my clothes and shoes from last night. "Coming!" I shouted back at the door.

Eddie did the same, and we ran out of our bedroom and to the suite door. I threw it opened just as the satyr was in mid-knock. "Sorry, Gunther," I said. "It totally slipped my mind."

He gave a sly smile. "Well, meeting with Doctor Orlok would 'slip' my mind as well."

We walked hurriedly beside him to the elevator. "I take it you don't care for Doctor Orlok," I observed.

He grimaced. "Let's just say we have different views on morality. Ever since your great-great-grandmother knighted him and granted him the position of Minister of Virtue, he believes everyone should adhere to his definition of ethics. Now, it's a fifteen-minute carriage ride to the Melbourne House."

"Oh, we'll make it there in five," Eddie said confidently. "I'll go get my motorcycle from the shed." Once we got down to the castle's main floor, I said goodbye to Gunter and quickly followed my husband out to the shed, which was the temporary parking place for his favorite mode of transportation. We put on our helmets, and Eddie turned over the engine as we climbed on.

In the land of the undead, there are two stages of daylight. Twilight: the morning and afternoon period where the sun never goes above the horizon, and your basic dark night. You'd think the sky would be bleak and grey, but no, it is a deep purple-orange hue. The mornings and afternoons were like twelve-hour sunsets. No vampire is ever in danger of sun damage to his or her skin.

He sped towards the closed, cedar gates looming before us. My husband can change into a green mist and perform a few magical spells, but none of those abilities would open any kind of gates.

"Uh, Eddie?"

"I got it." He pressed a brand new button in the middle of

9
8
7
6
5
4
3
2
1
1
2
3
4
5
6
7
8

the instrument panel, and the gates swung open. He shot a grin at me as we sped through. "Automatic gate opener." He closed the gates after us.

"How did you get one of those?"

"Archer gave me one. I'm going to get a couple more for our cars."

"Which are where?"

"In Cassius' hanger. He said I could keep them there until I get a garage built."

"And where is this garage of yours going to go?"

"I'm still trying to figure that out."

"Okay."

We rode down the mountain and through poorly lit, pothole-covered streets in the middle of town, and I waved to the shopkeepers opening up their businesses for the day. Signs proudly displaying their undying allegiance to the new queen and discounts fit for royalty. Ah, capitalism!

We rode on past buildings of all shapes and sizes and an audacious, Vegas-style casino smack-dab in the middle of the quaint downtown set in the hilly terrain of the island. The next road we turned down was the industrial part on Peregrine's docks. Huge smokestacks puffed out pollutants from various factories and mills. We drove past Cassius' airship hanger and a giant clock tower before turning left on the clean, two-mile-long driveway to the Melbourne Building.

"Wow!" I said the second I saw the building. It was as if someone had removed the dome on the United States capitol building and replaced it with one of the onion-shaped domes on Saint Basil's Cathedral. The blue and gold colors of the building sparkled in the twilight. Eddie parked off to the left side of the gold-plated, marble stairs.

As we walked up the steps, I couldn't take my eyes off the ten towering pillars flanking the entrance. Each one represented a gigantic replica of a member of various races in the hundred islands. An elf, vampire, satyr, centaur, sphinx, Welkie, werewolf, fairy, lamia, and Winged One each held up the neoclassical roof overshadowing the steps.

Two uniformed dwarves stood guard on either side of the twenty-foot, bronze doors. They wore white uniforms with double golden stripes running down each pant leg. On top of their shaved heads were red berets with an insignia of a blue lion surrounded by three fleurs-de-lis. As we approached, both men raised their assault rifles at Eddie and me. "Halt! Who goes there?" one shouted.

Before anyone could answer, the doors slowly swung open, and a middle-aged vampire stood in the threshold. Oh, my God, Shelly! Eddie said telepathically. It's Vincent Price in a three-piece Armani suit and a cape!

My husband was right. Either the master of horror movies had become a vampire, or this guy doubled as an impersonator. His graying black hair was swept back in an inch-high widow's peak. His gray eyes studied me warily, trying to determine just how good of a queen I would be, according to his rigidly high standards of morality and ethics. The vampire finally spoke, to my delight, with a perfect tone and inflection of Vincent Price's voice. "Stand down and bow to your Majesty, Queen Michelle!" he ordered the two dwarves.

Both men hurriedly dropped their weapons, fell to their knees, and groveled for several, awkwardly long seconds. "Okay, you can get up now," I told them. They obediently collected themselves and their weapons before standing aside to let us pass.

The tall, thin vampire introduced himself as Vincent Orlok,

Ph.D. "Your Highness, I trust you memorized your speech for this morning's coronation."

"Ah, about that," I started to say when Orlok cut me off.

"What are you wearing?"

I glanced down at my red Doctor Who T-shirt, wrinkled jeans, and sneakers. Not exactly coronation attire, but this was practice. "Clothes."

"The queen should always be dressed regally," Orlok said haughtily. "Her subjects must recognize her status among the rabble."

"No one likes being referred to as 'rabble,' Doctor," Eddie said.

Orlok ignored Eddie and stared right at me. "I hope, your Majesty, you have practiced your speech."

"Yeah, about that," I started to say, but the "good" doctor cut me off.

"I don't know you, but I believe that my words reflect your sentiments exactly. This queendom rose greatly under Queen Rachel. We kept foreigners out, built up the military, and increased the economic stability of the islands. Your sister did have a few faults, though. But I think you both share the same ideals."

Attempted sororicide. That would top the fault list. "My sister and I are very different," I said with an edge in my voice. "Do not compare us. Ever."

"I apologize, your Majesty."

"It's okay. Don't worry about it."

Orlok began to look around. "Where is your Guardian? A queen should never be without her Guardian."

Eddie stepped forward and put his arm around my waist. "That'd be me, Eddie Van Helsing." He leaned forward and shook Doctor Orlok's hand.

Orlok pulled back his hand as if my husband was diseased. "Do not touch the Minister of Virtue's hand, Guardian!" he snapped. "You're not supposed to interact with the queen's cabinet members. Your only duty is to protect the queen." He glared at Eddie's arm wrapped around my waist. "Not to have intimate relations with her."

"Yes, I can," Eddie said.

"Your Majesty, I must insist that you stop your relations

with your Guardian. Think of the scandals!"

"Not going to happen," I said.

"And why is that?" Orlok demanded.

"Because Eddie and I are very much married."

A look of shock registered across Orlok's face. "Forgive me, Your Highness." Finally, he looked Eddie straight in the eye. "Have you gone through the proper procedure to attain Guardian status?"

"What procedure?" Eddie asked.

Orlok struggled not to roll his eyes in front of his queen. "Every Guardian must complete an intensive, six-week training program with Master Joab to even be considered for the position."

"Wait a minute," I said. "Eddie's already my Guardian." I looked at my husband. "You don't need to go through any training."

"He does, or you must choose another Guardian," Orlok stated. "There are several others who are extremely qualified."

"No way, Eddie is the only person I trust with my life. He is my Guardian, and that will not change. He doesn't need to do the training."

"I'll do it," Eddie said. "It can't be any worse than my training with the Agency."

"Well, you must make a public announcement to choose your Guardian during the coronation," Orlok said. "Normally, it's the prime minister's job, but I shall have to take on that burden."

I thought for a brief moment before looking at Eddie. "How about I make you a temporary Guardian, and once you complete your training, I'll make another public announcement to make you my official Guardian. Would that work?"

"Sure!" Eddie said.

Orlok gave a melodramatic sigh. "I suppose that would be sufficient enough. Let's walk through the coronation." He beckoned us to follow him inside the building.

We headed down a short hall plastered with golden hanging flags depicting the Peregrin coat of arms before Orlok threw open the double, solid oak doors at the end of the corridor.

"This is the Forum," he said with an over-the-top car salesman wave encompassing the large room. It was shaped like a horseshoe with four hundred wooden seats with red leather backing. In front of each row of seats were long, dark red plastic tables equipped with microphones for every seat's occupants. In the middle of the horseshoe was a large, seven-foot-long carpeted stage with a wooden podium in the center. Behind the rostrum were three chairs.

Orlok saw me looking at the middle one. "Ah, I see you like your throne."

"Sure," I lied. The truth was I hated it. "Is it made out of solid gold?"

"Oh, yes! It was originally silver, but Queen Rachel had it refinished in gold. Do you like how the purple and blue diamonds are decorating the top?"

"It's colorful!" I said. Maybe the comfortability would overcome the tackiness. "Can I try it out now?"

"Of course!" He led us down to the stage. "Have a seat, your Highness."

I settled down on the throne. My suspicions were confirmed. The throne was as comfortable as those hard, plastic desk-chairs I was forced to sit in all through high school. I got up quickly from my seat. I may be immortal, but I wasn't about to endure centuries of searing back pain from ergonomically incorrect chairs. "I'm not going to have to sit in this for long periods, right?"

"Of course you do, your Highness. Every one of your ancestors has ruled from this very throne. You will carry on that tradition just as the prophecy had foretold."

Great, I thought, a thousand years of perpetual back problems. I decided to enforce my royal duties. "I want the throne to be used for special occasions. For the rest of the time, I want to be sitting in a more comfortable chair."

Orlok tried to sputter out an objection but gave up rather quickly. "If you insist, your Highness."

"I do."

"We should start the rehearsal." And we did. The Minister of Virtue called onto the stage a group of fifteen giggling kindergartners led by a red-headed plump vampire woman in a plain, black dress.

She pulled out a silver whistle hanging off a matching chain, tucked in her impressive cleavage, and blew four, long shrill whistles. "Attention!" she shouted at the children in an equally shrill voice. They immediately fell silent and quickly lined up.

Orlok smiled at her with admiration. "This is my wife, Prudence. She is the musical director at Peregrin School for the Gifted. Her students will be singing 'Queen and Country,' Peregrin's national anthem."

Prudence came over to me and bowed. "Your Highness, I know you will enjoy my students' song."

Twelve long verses later, which sounded more like a funeral dirge than a rousing national anthem, we thankfully went on with the next part of the rehearsal. The children were ushered off the stage, and the professor took their place. Orlok began his speech about the history of Peregrin. "Five thousand years ago, the queendom of Peregrin was founded by Queen Aquila and King Hermes. . ."

Eddie casually checked his watch for the fifth time. *He's been going on for fifty minutes*, he telepathically told me.

Fifty-one, I corrected.

I feel like I've been listening to someone read an

encyclopedia article. What's he talking about now?

I zoned out forty-five minutes ago. I glanced at Orlok. *Oh, look, he's wrapping up.* I focused my diverted attention back on the boring vampire.

". . .Now the prophecy has been fulfilled by our new queen, Michelle Van Helsing." He beckoned me. "You will now step forward and kneel before me."

I did.

Orlok opened up a large, rectangular box he pulled out from under the throne. He took out a large, golden crown covered in sapphires, a matching, two-foot-long standard scepter like the ones you'd see in movies, and a six-foot-long, cobalt robe.

I touched the soft, thick white fur trim on the robe. "Wow, this is soft. What kind of animal is this?"

"Polar bear," Orlok said.

And that would explain the lack of polar bears around here. We began swearing into the royal office.

"Will you solemnly promise and swear to govern the Peoples and Lands of Peregrin, according to their respective laws and customs?"

"I do?" I was unsure of what to say.

"Actually, your Highness, the correct phrase is 'I solemnly promise to do so.'"

"Sorry."

Orlok sighed and mumbled something about my ignorance before continuing. "Will you commit to your power cause Law and Justice, in Mercy, to be executed in all your judgments?"

"I solemnly promise to do so."

"The next phrase is 'All this I promise to do. The things which I have here before promised, I will perform and keep.' Then I will place the robe and crown on you and say, "I bestow the royal crown and robe to our new Queen Michelle. May you serve our people well.' Then you appoint your Guardian." He looked at Eddie. "And what is your name?"

"Eddie Van Helsing," my husband replied, frustration on the rise.

"Is that your full name?" Orlok asked with a hint of disgust."

"It's Edgar, but no one ever calls me that."

"All right, Edgar, the oath of the Guardian is very important. Have you memorized it?"

"Kind of," Eddie said. "I didn't have much time due to all the packing."

Orlok sighed again. We were definitely not scoring any points with the Minister of Virtue. "The oath goes, 'I, (insert your name here) pledge my service and life to her majesty, Queen Michelle, ruler of Peregrin. I swear to serve and protect her and place my duty to her before all else until the day I die in the Queen's service.' Then the queen will say, 'I, Queen Michelle, appoint Edgar Van Helsing, as my Guardian.'"

"What do I appoint him with?" I asked.

"The scepter. Please say your lines."

Eddie and I parroted the words back to Orlok. "Okay, what's next?" I asked.

"Your acceptance speech. I trust you've memorized it?"

"I'm working on it, Professor Orlok."

Eddie shot me a knowing glance. I wasn't going to memorize Orlok's five-page speech. I had thrown together a short speech I had written last week. The final step of the

coronation was a musical accompaniment as the people left the

stage.

Orlok strongly suggested we practice the ceremony three

more times. Mercifully, he took my advice to skip both the

painfully boring speech and song. With those two elements cut

out, the practice was only twenty minutes long.

Chapter Three:
The Coronation Crasher

After we got back to the castle, Eddie and I got ready for the day. Fully dressed, I was blow-drying my hair in the bathroom while my husband whipped up five-cheese omelets for us. Because I can't cook to save myself, he is the master chef in our household.

I shut off the hairdryer and came out into the kitchen, where Eddie was leaning against the counter and involved in an animated conversation with Gunther. The smell of sulfur was in the air. "Honey," I said, pointing to the black globs once representing eggs that were currently congealing into the frying pan, "our breakfast!" My husband obviously didn't hear me. I took upon it myself and turned off the stove. I let out a sad sigh. I was really looking forward to an omelet.

"Absolutely not!" Eddie said firmly.

"But it's tradition, Sir Eddie," the satyr said. "Each Guardian must wear this uniform during his or her swearing-in ceremony." Draped over his arms was the most ridiculous outfit I had ever seen in my life. The poofy, white shirt had an enormous, circular ruffled collar. Over the shirt was a blue and gold striped vest with golden epaulets on each shoulder. To accompany this hideous arrangement was a blue and gold striped M.C. Hammer pants that tapered off at the ankle.

"No, I'd rather wear a cape!" Eddie said.

Gunther gave me a weary look. "Your highness, can you please tell him he will only have to wear this outfit only once? I know it's a hideous outfit, Sir Eddie."

"Eddie, it can't be that bad," I said, taking in the audacious outfit once again. "I like the beret." The front of the red beret had a blue lion surrounded by three fleurs-de-lis pinned on the front. "Just wear it. How bad can it be?"

Eddie sighed in defeat. "At least, let me wear my brown dress shoes to save some small amount of my dignity." He pointed to the brown cloth shoes with the blue and gold

pom-pom at the top of the toes Gunther had set down.

"I agree," I replied. "Those shoes have to go."

The satyr sighed. "All right. Your Highness, let me show

your coronation dress."

"What dress?" This was the first time I had heard my outfit

was going to pick out for me. Gunther set Eddie's outfit next to

the dress currently lying across the kitchen table. It was a blue

dress with shoulder pads as big as a couch. There was

absolutely no neckline, courtesy of the barbette. The white linen

medieval-style headdress was supposed to cover my entire head

and neck, leaving only the face visible.

I touched the fabric and sighed. The headpiece and the

dress were about as flexible as a two-by-four and just as soft. A

two-hour coronation in uncomfortable clothing. Fantastic. I

picked up the dress and turned it around. A golden bow the size

of a minivan stretched across the back of the waistline. Oh god, I

was going to be crowned in a medieval style, 80's prom dress.

A thought came to Eddie. "Will these fit us?" he asked.

"Oh, yes," Gunther said. "The fabric of both your outfits is made from the leaves of the munco tree. Your clothes will magically adjust to your body."

Oh, crap! Eddie and I thought at the same time.

"I will leave you to get dressed. The coronation begins in two hours." Gunther bowed to me and left our suite.

I sighed. "So much for the purple dress that I bought last week."

Eddie was about to dump the blackened eggs when he began to look around. "Did you pack our kitchen wastebasket?"

I stopped rooting through the empty cupboards and looked at my husband. "No, it was dirty. Why would we bring a used wastebasket?"

"Sorry, I'm running on a few hours of sleep." He looked back at the skillet in his hand. "Where to put this?" He asked more to himself than to me. He made a decision and set the pan back on the cooled down burner.

My stomach growled. "Maybe we can order room service." Someone knocked on the door to our suite. "Come in!" I called out.

Rupert opened the door and pushed in a service cart. On

top of it sat a covered silver tray, two tall, crystal glasses, and a pitcher of orange juice. "Good morning, your Highness and Mr. Van Helsing. The cook thought you would like some breakfast before your coronation." The centaur lifted the cover of the tray. The aroma of creamed eggs on Italian toast and fresh banana bread filled the air, driving me crazy with hunger.

"Oh, yes. That'd be great!" Eddie said, a little too enthusiastically. He looked at me for agreement.

"Definitely!" I said.

"Then I'll leave the cart here," Rupert said. "Shall I send in Master Joab?"

"Who?" I asked.

"Mr. Van Helsing's Guardian trainer," our butler replied. "He's been waiting for the past few minutes."

"Sure." I got up, grabbed the two plates full of food, and carried them to the kitchen table after Eddie cleared our ceremonial outfits off the table and onto the nearby couch. I made a mental note to move the sofa out of the kitchen and into the living room. Eddie poured orange juice into both glasses and joined me at the table.

Rupert bowed to me, backed out of the suite with practiced ease, and announced Master Joab.

A short vampire with the built of a fire hydrant came into the kitchen. His steel-gray hair was trimmed in a buzz-cut style. His spotless, long-sleeved white dress shirt was tucked into a pair of navy blue dress pants with a thick, gold stripe running the length of each pant leg. His black shoes shone with fresh polish. He gave a brisk bow. "Your Majesty," he said in a serious voice, "I'm Joab Bloodhound, a former Guardian and a Guardian trainer. You may call me 'Master Joab.' I understand you and your chosen Guardian have a unique situation."

I nodded as I finished the piece of toast on my fork. "Yes, this is my chosen Guardian, my husband, Eddie Van Helsing."

Master Joab looked at Eddie with harboring doubt in his stoic dark brown eyes. My husband was not what he had expected. The Guardian trainer had been looking forward to training someone like himself, a military man, definitely not a mild-mannered vampire in faded jeans, a red Aerosmith T-shirt, and running shoes. Master Joab looked back at me. "Why him?"

I speared another piece of toast with my fork. "Eddie's the

only person I trust to watch my back." It didn't take a telepath like me to see that he wasn't convinced. "Also, he has saved my life on many occasions," I added.

Master Joab stared at Eddie with unflinching eyes. "What qualifies you to be a Guardian, young man?" He almost shouted the question like a drill sergeant.

Eddie could have proclaimed his love, dedication, and loyalty for me (which I would've appreciated,) but instead, he finished his orange juice slowly before speaking. "I spent over twenty years with an international spy organization, known as the Agency, and ten years as a bounty hunter, and then eight years of various odd jobs, some of which were bodyguard jobs."

"So, you have no experience then." Probably just some pencil pusher in a government agency, the Guardian trainer thought.

"No," Eddie corrected. "Just some experience as a field agent."

Master Joab attempted to suppress an aggravated sigh. "I take it you have already made your choice, your Highness." He gave Eddie a cursory glance. "I suppose you'll have to do,

Master Eddie. Training will start at 3:00 this afternoon at my training facility. Do not be late!" After giving Eddie a business card, he gave me a stiff bow and exited our suite.

Eddie finished off his breakfast and dumped his dishes into the sink. "He seems okay. Doesn't he, Shell?"

I didn't answer at first but got up and went to the fridge in search of blood. Maybe the refrigerator pixies came in the middle of the night and restocked. I swung open the door and stared at the almost empty shelves in dismay. At least I had my blood. I reached for a bottle of red fruit dragon blood, unscrewed the cap, and took a few swallows. "Hate to break it to you, Eddie, but Master Joab doesn't think you're up to the challenge."

"How could he think that? He barely knows me."

I would have offered him a sip from my blood bottle, but my husband has a rare, genetic blood allergy. If he ingests one drop of blood, he gets very sick. According to statistics, one out of every one-thousand vampires is allergic to blood. Blood for vampires is more of a dietary supplement than a daily requirement. To compensate for his blood intolerance, Eddie is a vegetarian. I took another sip of my strawberry-dipped-in-honey flavored blood. "Okay, I read his mind, and Master Joab was expecting you to be more militant and have more experience. He also thinks you were a pencil-pusher with the Agency."

Eddie was outraged at the accusation. "I was one of the Agency's top spies! I spent ten years capturing elusive, notorious criminals. I've fought zombie clowns, mummies, book demons, dinosaurs, doppelgängers, gargoyles, and sorcerers."

I could've corrected my husband by reminding him that I fought alongside him with all those things. I kept quiet and didn't spoil his tirade.

"You know what, Shelly?" he asked but didn't give me time to answer. "I'm definitely up for the challenge. I'll be the best Guardian Master Joab has ever trained. In fact, I will complete the training in half its normal time."

Once Eddie takes on a task, there is no stopping him. "Go for it, honey," I encouraged.

"Oh, I will." He decided to change the subject and asked about my speech.

"Well, I think I've got it down pat. Want to hear it?"

He nodded. Once I recited my new speech to him, he

looked at his watch. "Not even a minute, babe. I'm impressed."

"Well, I figured no one wants a long, insincere speech. Most people appreciate short, memorable speeches."

"Well, it's a lot better than Doctor Orlok's pretentious speech."

"I should hope so," I glanced at my watch. "We should get dressed."

Eddie glanced at his flamboyant outfit. "Do we have to?"

"Unfortunately." I gathered up the dress and went into our bedroom with Eddie following me. With my back to Eddie, I peeled out of my shirt and pants and pulled on a pair of nylons and a short black slip I had laid out on our mattress earlier. I took the barbette and stared at it, wishing it came with instructions. I started to ask my husband how to put it on when I saw him. I covered my mouth as I began doubling over in laughter.

"Very funny," Eddie said. He was threading the matching striped belt through the loops on his audacious pants. Nobody looks good in a poofy pirate shirt and striped vest with those shoulder tassels.

"You look like a Thespian actor who got lost in a marching

band," I said, once I gained control of my laughter.

He tugged at the rough collar. "This thing is slicing into my neck!" He brushed off a piece of non-existent lint on the golden tassels. He placed the beret on his head.

"The beret looks good on you, honey," I said, honestly. I finally figured out the barbette, placed it correctly (veil in back, not in front) on my head, and adjusted the strap. I unzipped my dress and climbed into it. I managed to zip the dress halfway. I could feel the magical fabric closing in around my body, but to my relief, I wasn't suffocated. The fabric adjusted to my size. I wanted all my clothes to be made from this stuff.

"The hat is the only part of the outfit I do like." Eddie finished zipping up my dress. When I turned around, it was his turn to laugh.

"Is it as bad as I think it is?" I asked him.

"No, not at all, babe," he lied between fits of laughter. "You know what your dress reminds me of."

"What?"

"The time I went undercover as a high school prom chaperone back in 1983."

"What type of assignment would involve a high school prom?"

"It really wasn't an official assignment. The Director asked me to guard his daughter at her senior prom."

"Let me guess. He didn't like the guy she was with."

He nodded. He finally stopped laughing. "I'm sorry, Shelly, but that dress is—."

"I know." I managed to glance at the sofa-size shoulder pads and the equally large bow in the back. Usually, I try to look for positive aspects in outfits, but this dress was a complete disaster. "I hate this dress."

Eddie sat on the edge of the mattress and put on his brown dress shoes. "We only have to wear these outfits for today."

"Thank God," I said. I picked up an old, red leather-bound book on the floor next to Eddie's feet. Written across the cover in silver lettering were the phrases: Knowledge is Power. Without Knowledge, There is no Power. I said the first phrase, and green sparks of magic swirled around the book as it morphed into a sheathed sixteen-inch blade sword complete with a black nylon belt that could be worn over my back or around my waist. I went for the waist option.

The very last thing I put on was a mental bracelet similar to the ones Wonder Woman wears. But this one has a small button on the bracelet's underside. Once pressed and locked into place, the switch activates an impenetrable metal shield that pops out of the bracelet. I called my sword Knowledge and my shield Truth.

"Expecting trouble?" Eddie asked.

"No, but it doesn't hurt to be prepared."

Eddie lifted up his right pant leg to reveal his Scorpion XL, a high caliber gun with laser bullets, in an ankle holster. "True, and these pants are great for concealed weapons. Not that I would ever willingly wear these pants in public."

We heard a knock on our suite door. We left the bedroom and opened the suite door. "Gunther, what is it?" I asked.

The satyr burst out, laughing at the sight of us. He quickly regained his composure. "I'm so sorry, Your Highness, but—."

"It's all right, Gunther," I said. "Let it out."

"I forgot how ridiculous those outfits are," Gunther said.

He wore a double-breasted charcoal grey suit and a black bowler hat. "I want to show to the royal stables where you'll take a coach to the Melbourne House," he said.

"All right," I said. "Lead on." Eddie and I followed Gunther to the elevator.

"How was rehearsal?" Gunther asked us as he pressed the main floor elevator button.

"Excruciatingly long," Eddie answered.

"Doctor Orlok gave his history of the queendom?" Gunther guessed.

"I've got more excitement out of reading an encyclopedia article," I said.

"Did you like our national anthem?"

"Sure," I lied. "I've always liked funeral dirges."

Gunther smiled at my sarcasm. "I keep telling Mrs. Orlok to rewrite the national anthem. She refuses, saying something about keeping with tradition. She doesn't like the suggestions I gave."

"You write music?"

The satyr smiled in embarrassment. "It's a hobby of mine.

I'm not that good."

"What type of music do you write?" Eddie asked.

"Jazz."

"That's awesome," I said. "Would you mind showing us some of your work sometime?"

"Of course." Gunther led us out of the elevator and the brand-new main doors of Castle DeLorean. The courtyard stables were only a few yards away, right next to the shed. I was shocked at how small the stables seemed next to the castle itself. The elongated, two-story building is painted a dark green with white trim.

"The stables seem kind of small, don't they?" I asked my private secretary.

"They're sufficient enough to house the six royal winged unicorns and three royal carriages," Gunther replied. He opened up the stable doors, and instantly the three of us were bathed in eight rows of fluorescent lights hangings from eight rafters. Eight large stables were on either side of the barn. Bridles, saddles, and all kinds of riding equipment hung on the wall outside of each stable. Bits of hay and feed were scattered across the cement floor. In the last three stables were three large carriages. "Ohmigod, Eddie!"

Eddie stared in slack-jawed amazement. "These things are great!" Indeed, they were. The three carriages were shaped like coconuts, and the wheels were shaped like round orange slices. There were six windows on each carriage. Two of them were on either side of the carriage's two doors. The other two windows were in the front (so you can see the driver) and the back.

"Can you open the carriage windows?" I asked.

"Yep!" Out from behind one of the carriages stepped a tall, rugged Winged One in a plaid shirt and overalls. His steel-toed boots were covered in hay and winged unicorn manure. Two magnificent, six-foot-long, red-feathered wings sprouted from his broad shoulders. He took off his leather work gloves and shook my hand with one of his huge, calloused hands. "Name's Horace, yer Majesty," he introduced himself.

"Nice to meet you, Horace," I said. "I'm Princess Shelly, and this is my husband and Guardian, Eddie Van Helsing."

Eddie and Horace exchanged handshakes and hellos.

Horace noticed me looking at the winged unicorns. "Beautiful critters, aren't they?" he asked.

"Oh, yes, they are," I agreed. I had never seen winged unicorns before, and I was impressed. The black unicorns with their silver, two-foot-long horns looked like Clydesdales on steroids. Their rainbow-colored manes and tails were in pristine condition. I reached out to stroke the white starred nuzzle of the unicorn closest to me. "Hey, there," I told it.

Before anyone could warn me, the unicorn bared its sharp teeth at me and nearly severed my fingers. I took a few quick steps back out of the range of the unicorn's head. Note to self: Don't pet the royal winged unicorns.

"Yeah," Horace drawled, "they don't take well to strangers." He reached up and petted the unicorn, who whinnied happily in return. "This here's Alpha," He pointed to a unicorn with a thick orange streak down his nose. "That's Omega," "That's Beta, Delta, Epsilon, and Gamma," he introduced the other unicorns to us. He walked over to the nearest carriage and pushed it outside the stables. Eddie, Gunther, and I followed him and climb inside. "I'll go get Alpha and Omega," he said as he headed back inside.

Eddie opened the carriage door and did a quick safety inspection around the carriage. "All clear, Shelly," he said as he climbed in.

I smiled. "Thanks, Eddie." I placed my foot on the carriage's step and looked back over my shoulder at the satyr. He was heading back to the castle. "Gunther, are you coming?"

His eyes widened in complete surprise. "Oh, no, I can't. Only the royal family and their Guardians are allowed in the royal carriages."

"Don't worry about it. Come on!"

He hesitated. "I don't want to be a bother."

I beckoned him in. "I insist," I said with a smile. "Anyway, I need someone to tell me who I'll be rubbing elbows with at the banquet."

Gunther smiled appreciatively as he followed me inside the carriage. He sat on one of navy blue, two-seat velvet cushions across from Eddie and me. He crossed his legs and leaned against the window facing the driver's seat. "Well, you might meet the Prime Minister at the banquet."

I glanced out the side window and was surprised to see the ground a good 500-feet below the carriage. The streetlights flicked below like lighting bugs under the glow of the twilight sky. "Wow, we're up in the air already."

"Yes, the winged unicorns are powerful and very swift animals," Gunther said. He glanced over at Eddie, who was cautiously looking out the window. "Is everything all right, Master Eddie?"

"Oh, yeah, I'm just not a fan of flying anything controlled by animals."

"Oh," Gunther answered, confused by my husband's answer.

"Eddie trusts mechanics more than animals," I explained. "So, what's the prime minister like?"

"I don't know. He hasn't been seen for several years."

"What you mean you haven't seen him in several years?" I asked.

Gunther hesitated. "Where should I start?"

"The beginning's always a nice place," I replied.

"When the people of Peregrin were just a small clan, your

ancestor, Queen Aquila, found Hiram. He had been injured when he fell from his realm to this realm. She and King Hermes nursed him back to health. As a reward, he flew to an asteroid and collected a firestone as a gift. Over seven hundred years, the queendom received seven firestones from Hiram. Then the queen offered him the position as prime minister."

"Okay," I said, "what's the problem?"

"There was a disagreement about the firestones, and Hiram left," Gunther answered before quickly changing the conversation. "At the banquet, you will meet the rest of your cabinet and answer a few of their questions. Senator Hamish Lionheart, the minister of state, wants to know the queendom's five-year plan. Reggie Loup, the minister of finance, needs to give you a report on the queendom's financial state." Gunther was avoiding the prime minister topic like the bubonic plague. I tried to press the issue further, but the satyr kept silent, despite my prodding.

Within moments and no further explanation about Hiram's absence from Gunther, we landed outside Melbourne's steps.

We got out and were greeted by surprised stares from the people entering the building. Apparently, only members of the royal family were supposed to ride in carriages, not the servants.

"Good morning, Cassius," I said to a stocky, six-foot vampire with a black patch over his right eye as he ascended the marble steps towards us.

The captain of the airship Monte Carlo had traded-in his signature 1940's black leather jacket and black dress pants with the single red stripe down the legs for a black tuxedo. He still wore his red beret over his military-style black hair. On the front of the beret was a blue lion surrounded by three fleurs-de-lis. "You look—." He struggled for the right, non-insulting words to compliment my dress and not get himself in trouble.

Dr. Orlok pushed his way in front of Cassius. He still wore his expensive suit under a blue and gold robe similar to college professors' graduation day garments. An audacious golden bubble beret with a blue pompom the size of a softball sat atop the Minister of Virtue's head. "Come, come, your Highness, the coronation about to start," he said impatiently. Then he said in a low voice, "You must learn not to mingle with commoners."

I looked at Orlok squarely in the eyes. "I will mingle with whomever I please."

"Yes, your Highness," Orlok sulked. "You, Private Secretary," he said to Gunther, "I believe there might be balcony seating available." He then made a shooing motion with his hands at the satyr.

Gunther shot him eye-daggers before giving me a respectful bow. As he left us, I could hear him calling Orlok something very unkind under his breath.

Orlok was too full of himself to hear Gunther's insults. He led Eddie and me to the Forum. The large room was filled wall-to-wall with well-dressed people, both rich and poor. The throng parted without hesitation as the Minister of Virtue strutted like a rooster down the center aisle. The room was strangely quiet. You could literally hear a pin drop. Coronations were supposed to be happy, not solemn. We climbed onto the platform. Three men and a woman sat in a row of six fancy high back chairs surrounding my uncomfortable throne.

I sat on my throne, and Eddie stood off to my right, just as Orlok had instructed us. I nodded a smile at the Ministers.

Gunther told me who they were, but I couldn't remember any of their names for the life of me. The only other person on stage I recognized was Nessa Wolfsguard, the general of Peregrin's small but formidable military. The werewolf in her wolf form wore a black suit with golden stripes running down each pant leg. Sitting on her wedge-cut raven hair was a red beret with my queendom's symbol. She gave me a curt nod when our eyes met.

Then the boring coronation began. The children's singing was barely tolerable. Ninety-percent of the crowd fell asleep during Orlok's history lesson, while the other ten percent discreetly checked emails or send texts on their cellphones. On the other hand, I couldn't do either because the paparazzi were blinding me with their camera flashes.

". . .Now the prophecy has been fulfilled by our new queen, Michelle Van Helsing." Orlok's closing statements had barely registered with me. A long moment passed before the Minister of Virtue cleared his throat in a not-at-all subtle manner.

"Sorry," I whispered as I shot up from my uncomfortable

throne. I walked over to where Orlok was standing by a clear plastic lectern. I remembered to kneel before the vampire shot me an aggravated look.

He took out the crown and robe from the box next to the lectern. "Will you solemnly promise and swear to govern the Peoples and Lands of Peregrin, according to their respective laws and customs?"

"I solemnly promise to do so."

"Will you, in your power, uphold Law and Justice with Mercy, to be carried out in all your judgments?"

"All this I promise to do. These things which I have here before promised, I will perform and keep." I gave myself a mental high five for actually remembering the exact wording.

He placed the heavy robe on my shoulders, and immediately my body temperature rose fifty degrees. Then he lowered the crown on my head and said, "I bestow the royal crown, scepter, and robe to our new Queen Michelle. May you serve our people well. Arise, Queen Michelle." He lightly but overdramatically touched both my shoulders with the scepter before giving it to me.

I slowly got to my feet. Not because I was trying to be dignified. I didn't want to throw off my balance. I looked to Orlok for the next step.

"Now, Queen Michelle will choose her Guardian. Guardian, step forward and kneel before your queen."

Eddie came forward and got down on one knee. I smiled, remembering the day he proposed to me. He had asked me to be his wife, and now he was publicly accepting his new position as my Guardian. He looked up at me and smiled. "I, Edgar Van Helsing, pledge my service and life to her majesty, Queen Michelle, ruler of Peregrin. I swear to serve and protect her and place my duty to her before all else until the day I die in the Queen's service." His confident voice never wavered. He then respectfully bowed his head.

A bubble of pride swelled up in me. "I, Queen Michelle, appoint Edgar Van Helsing as my Guardian." I lightly tapped both his shoulders with the scepter, visually sealing the deal.

I placed my hands on the lectern and looked out across the throng of people eagerly awaiting my coronation speech. Taking a deep breath, I took four index cards out of my dress pocket and placed them on the podium. "My fellow Peregrines, I humbly and graciously accept my new role as your queen. Like my mother, grandmother, and the other queens before me, I have extraordinary examples to follow. Even this will be a new and wonderful experience for all of us. I realize my accession to the throne has come at a difficult time in our nation's history. We will not heal overnight. We will not heal by next week, but we will heal. How will we do this, you ask? By no longer hiding in the shadows from our fellow nations, by sharing our valuable resources with our neighbors, by mending fences with enemies and making new allies."

I glanced over at Eddie. "My husband shares and respects my ideals, and I hope you will as well. I want to hear your thoughts and ideas about Peregrin so you can contribute to the building up of our nation. A queen does not represent a country; the people do.

"Even though I'm a newcomer here, I realize how much my ancestors believed in and loved Peregrin. You are wonderful and kind people who believed in me when I did not believe in myself. For this, I thank you. I cannot and will not make any vain promises, but I promise this: I will do my best to rule Peregrin with kindness and integrity. Thank you." I stepped back, expecting roaring applause and hearty shouts of "All hail, Queen Michelle" to fill the room.

Instead, there was a loud BOOM as red smoke filled the stage. Something knocked the lectern over. It skittered towards the cabinet members and me. Eddie grabbed my shoulders and yanked me out of its path. Someone used a levitation spell to lift the careening lectern before it crashed into the reporters below.

The smoke cleared, and the strangest creature I had ever seen appeared. I know people with wings, so the colossal eagle wings sprouting from his back didn't surprise me, nor did his two eagle talons, which were leaving deep claw marks on the floor. What surprised me was the moose head sitting on top of his human body. Towering over us a good ten feet, he spoke with a loud, resonating voice that echoed throughout the room. I instantly drew my sword and activated my shield with just a press of the underside button. Eddie had dropped to his knees and quickly retrieved his gun from its ankle holster. "How dare you give these people false hope!" the stranger shouted at me.

"You don't even trust your own prime minister and falsely accuse him of a despicable crime! You are just like all the others!" With that, he vanished in a puff of red smoke.

The entire audience sat in stunned silence. I stepped forward and addressed them. "Was anyone hurt?" The question was answered by the shaking of heads and the murmurs of no's. I asked for an emergency meeting of my cabinet members back at the castle. I was going to get to the bottom of this, no matter what

Chapter Four:
I Go Where Royals Fear to Tread

Back in the pea soup green conference room of Castle DeLorean, I stood at the long, cherry table while my cabinet members seated themselves. Rupert brought in a tray of cheese and sliced fruit along with a pitcher of water and glasses. Gunther sat on my left with a notebook and pen in his hand, and Eddie sat on my right, pretending to look at his smartphone, but paying attention to every word. "Can someone please explain to me what just happened?" I asked.

Senator Hamish Lionheart looked anxiously at his fellow cabinet members before answering. Sitting next to him was the minister of agriculture, an elegant fairy named Peggy

Swallowtail. A centaur, Christabelle Shadowfax, who was the minister of commerce, stood next then Cassius and Doctor Orlok. "Well, your Majesty, there was a misunderstanding between your grandmother, Queen Melissa, and Hiram."

"Yeah, Mr. Hornicus mentioned it." I shot my secretary an annoyed look. "But he failed to go into detail."

The werelion ran his fingers through his golden mane in a nervous gesture. "The firestones went missing, and Hiram was accused of the theft."

"Did he do it?" I asked.

Doctor Orlok harrumphed. "Of course, he did. He wanted the firestones for himself."

Gunther raised his hand. "Hiram denied it. I remember him arguing with the king and queen."

"Of course, he denied it," Doctor Orlok insisted. "A criminal always claims innocence. Only a pamola could have broken into the sealed, magically-protected vault and stolen the firestones."

I looked at Chief Justice Ruhn Faunus, the Minister of Justice. "Was there a trial or an investigation?"

The satyr shook his head. "Unfortunately, no. Hiram left, and the queen didn't press charges. She had other things on her mind."

The others nodded as if remembering. Cassius, my minister of transportation, spoke cautiously. "I don't mean to dishonor your grandparents' memory, your Majesty." He paused and waited. I gave him a nod to continue. "On one of the islands, there were rumors of war against the main island. The islanders supposedly had made allies with some Level 5 demons. Queen Melissa wanted to attack the island. Hiram suggested negotiations to confirm the rumors, but she refused to listen to him. The island was attacked, but we learned too late demons had killed everyone in the town. That was the start of the Demon Wars." The entire room fell silent as they recollected the Demon Wars and the aftermath that followed.

"It would be nice to get the firestones back. The queendom's finances plummeted when they went missing," Reggie Loup, the werewolf Minister of Finance, explained.

"What do the firestones have to do with the financial state of Peregrin?" I asked.

"Well, each firestone is worth about 100 trillion dollars," Mr. Loup said.

Eddie nearly choked on the grape he had just popped in his mouth as my jaw dropped in surprise.

"I'm sorry," I said, "I must have heard wrong. Did you say '100 trillion?'"

Mr. Loup nodded. "How do you think the queendom survived being hidden from the rest of the world all this time?"

"Oh," I said. I thought about what I had just been told. Hiram was wrongfully accused of theft and still carried a grudge. That I understood. His actions at the coronation were another matter altogether. His temper tantrum could've killed someone. I made a decision. "Where does Hiram live?"

"In a cave on the southern side of Mount Hottah," Gunther said.

"Good. Cassius, can the Monte Carlo take us up there?"

The entire cabinet gasped in horror. Eddie put away his cell phone and stood next to me. "Calm down, everyone! The queen just wants to talk to him. She's not going to start a war. As her Guardian, I will be accompanying her so she will be safe."

"That settles it," I said. "Cassius?"

The airship captain stood. "I can have my airship ready within an hour and a half. Meet us at my hanger."

I should've known we were going to have problems meeting Hiram when Gunther suggested we arm ourselves. I still had Knowledge and Truth on me, and Eddie had his two handguns along with an array of other weapons. I went to the bottom floor of the castle. The bottom floor consisted of six rooms: the royal bunker with a private restroom, the war room, two gyms (one for the staff and one for the royals,) the security office, bathrooms, and the armory. I walked to the security office and knocked on the door.

A werewolf in a black security outfit opened the door. "Your Majesty, what can I do for you?" asked Archer Wulfsguard, Castle DeLorean's Head of Security.

"Could you unlock the armory for me?" I asked.

"Sure thing." He got up from his seat and walked with me over to the armory door. He pressed a series of numbers on a keypad before the metal door slid back into the wall with a slow

WOOSH.

Eddie and I stepped inside. Even though the room was twice the size of a walk-in closet, it didn't feel claustrophobic. The walls were lined with every kind of weapon imaginable. Every wall could open up and reveal a hidden wall equipped with even more weapons. "Archer, what would you recommend for a good, long-range weapon?"

"What do you need it for?"

"I'm going to have a little chat with Hiram."

Archer nodded. "I heard what happened at the coronation. Good thing, no one was hurt. It's funny, but I don't remember Hiram ever wanting to hurt the royal family."

"Really? Any recommendations for weaponry?"

"We have some excellent firearms."

"Do you have anything else? My shooting has the accuracy of a Star Wars Stormtrooper."

The werewolf smiled. "I think we can find something else." He walked to the back of the closet and opened up a hidden wall to revile a secret compartment lined with various crossbows. He removed a small semi-automatic pistol from a hostler and pulled back the hammer. The barrel split into two, revealing a crossbow armed with an arrow. "This might suit your fancy. My sister calls it 'the Porcupine.' Aims by itself and will never miss. Just point and pull the trigger. The best thing about this crossbow is its automatic reloading feature. A magical arrow will reappear every time."

Archer's sister, Nessa Wulfsguard, was the general of the Peregrin armed forces. Like all werewolves, General Wulfsguard and her brother each possess a magical ability. Archer can make a door appear anywhere. The general, a weapons expert, can conjure up any kind of weapon. This little weapon was undoubtedly one of her best.

"I'll take it," I said. Archer handed me the crossbow, and I clipped it to my belt near my sword. "Anything else you recommend?"

The werewolf nodded. He closed the hidden wall and stepped to the other side of the room. He took two metal rings about the size of Frisbees off the wall. "Chakrams. Deadly throwing rings. With a flick of the wrist, you can take out an enemy within 40-60 yards, and the chakrams will return to you."

"How hard are these things to throw?"

"Not hard at all. They'll find their mark no matter what."

I suspected Archer knew I needed idiot-proof weapons, but I said nothing. I clipped two hooks onto my belt before placing the chakrams on them.

Archer noticed Eddie looking at a grappling gun. "You can have it."

"Sweet," Eddie said as he took it off the shelf. "Anything else?"

Archer grabbed a shield bracelet similar to mine off a wall and handed it to my husband, who immediately put it on. Then the werewolf remembered something. He retrieved a golden baton with a ring of sapphires at the top and handed it to Eddie. "Every king has used Vengeance as his weapon of choice," he explained.

"Okay? Thanks?" Eddie said. He looked uncertainly at the golden baton. *What am I supposed to do with this? Beat someone with it?* He wondered.

"Give it a quick shake and slide that button with your thumb," Archer advised.

Eddie did so. The baton rapidly extended into a six-foot-long staff with a two-foot-long, slightly curved blade. I recognized the war scythe my husband had used to dispatch Diamondback. "This is perfect," Eddie said as he attempted to take a practice swing.

"Sire, not in the armory," Archer said as he and I both took a step backward from the swinging scythe.

Eddie apologized." How do I—?"

"Just do what you did before," Archer said.

He gave it another quick shake and slid back the button. The scythe collapsed back into the baton. "I think I've got everything I need. What about you, Shell?"

"I'm good," I said, "but we need to change our clothes. I certainly don't want to confront Hiram in my coronation outfit."

After going through three different outfits, I finally picked out a jade-colored dress shirt, black dress pants, and heavy-duty black dress shoes. Eddie changed into a black sports jacket over a red polo shirt, black dress pants, and leather dress shoes. He put on his weapons utility belt, adding the grappling gun and

Vengeance. "What's your plan?" Eddie asked me.

"First, we're going to have a little chat with Hiram," I said as we walked to the elevator. I pressed the second-floor button.

"And?"

"That's as far as my plan goes. I'm going to play the rest of it by ear."

The doors opened, and we stepped inside. Eddie pressed the button to the main floor. "Do you have an ultimate goal?"

"That I do have. Retrieve the firestones."

"At least we have an end goal. A first for us."

I looked at him with feigned shock. "My plans always have goals. Yes, those goals usually have us not getting killed."

"I'm just glad your plan has a different goal this time. It's nice to switch things up a bit."

Eddie had taken out his phone and was swiping his fingers across the screen. I glanced at the app he was using. "What are you doing?" I asked.

"Making blueprints for the royal helicopter," he said. He showed me a detailed, black-and-white outline of a helicopter on a light blue background. "It's just a basic blueprint. I'm going to talk with Cassius to see if he can help me build it."

I was so impressed with my husband. Within an hour, he had sketched out the plans to build a helicopter. It looked sleek and swift. Eddie is a mechanical genius. He can build any kind of vehicle, usually in the shape of fruits and vegetables. This time it was your standard design. "How come no fruits or vegetables this time?"

"I thought a basic design would be more appropriate for her Majesty," he said. "It's going to be a long-range helicopter, too."

Taxes were sky-high, to begin with, and I was pretty sure the citizens of Peregrin weren't going to be too thrilled with the new queen building a private helicopter. "Okay," I said as I attempted to do the cost calculations in my head. Once I reached one million, my brain was about to explode. I didn't want to disappoint him. "Okay, but make sure you keep the cost down."

Eddie gave me a kiss after putting away his phone. "Of course, I will. If it's too much, I won't build it."

"Uh-uh," I said sarcastically, "because by then, you'll forget all about it."

He laughed. "Actually, I thought we could use some of the money from the firestones to pay for the cost."

"Oh," I said, "but be sure to leave plenty for some of my ideas."

"What ideas?"

"Well, I want to restore the public library, build a couple of museums and a zoo, an aquarium, restore the military and sheriff's department, and rebuild the infrastructure here."

"Wow! That makes my helicopter plans seem selfish," he said with a grin.

"And I want to redecorate some of these rooms."

"Ah-ha!" Eddie pointed a finger. "So you do have some selfish plans for the firestones!"

"Did you notice the color of the conference room? It looks like someone threw up pea soup and called it a paint job."

The elevator door opened, and we got off on the main floor where Gunther met us. In his hands, he held a gigantic, leather-bound ledger with worn pages. He thrust the book into my hands. "Your Majesty, I highly recommend you read this. It's a ledger about the firestones' worth over the years."

"Okay, I'll read it on the flight over. How long will it take to get to Hiram's place?"

"About an hour," the satyr replied.

"See you later, Gunther," I told him.

"Good luck, your Majesties," he said as he started to walk away.

I looked at the ledger and tried to remember something from the one accounting class I took in high school. I recalled squat. *But I do have a private secretary*, I reminded myself. I called to the satyr. "Gunther?"

Gunther stopped and turned his head. "Yes, your Majesty?"

"I am terrible at all things mathematical. I was wondering if you would like to come with us and explain the ledger to me."

"Why yes! I would love to come."

We all walked out to the southeast corner of the courtyard where Eddie was currently parking his five cars. "Eddie, we're going to need to have a garage for all the vehicles," I told him as he unlocked his favorite one, a sleek, orange car in the shape of a carrot. We unloaded our weapons into the trunk before piling in and heading to the docks where Cassius' airplane hangar home was. The sixty-foot high metal semicircle-shaped structure towered over us as we pulled into the driveway. The roof was opened, and we could see half of the Monte Carlo's gray balloon bobbed up and down. Eddie pulled into the driveway and parked the car near the open double doors. Cassius greeted us at the door in his flight uniform and tipped his red beret to me. "I see you're all ready for the trip, your Majesty," he said.

"Yes," I said. "I hope we're not imposing on you and your crew."

"Of course not, We're glad to do it. It'll be an adventure," the airship captain said with a genuine smile. "Bring your car in the hangar. You can store it here for the time being."

Eddie went back and drove the car inside. He parked it out of the way and grabbed our weapons from the trunk. He walked over to where Gunther and I stood with Cassius.

The vampire captain pulled a walkie-talkie out of his panzer jacket's inside pocket and spoke into it. "Yancey, I need four teleportation spheres sent to my location."

"Yes, captain," replied a voice on the other end. Seconds later, four circular objects appeared in front of us. The rainbow colors shimmered as they hovered in midair. We all touched the spheres, and instantly we were teleported into the narrow, main hall of the *Monte Carlo.*

"Our flight time is an hour. Make yourselves comfortable," the captain said. He reached into his pocket and pulled out three earbuds. "These comlinks will work once you're off the *Monte Carlo*. They work just like walkie-talkies."

"Is your conference room available?" I asked as Eddie, Gunther, and I slipped the comlinks into our ears.

"Yes, it is. Right, this way." Cassius led the way to the conference room. The room was painted battleship gray with a long black conference table surrounded by eight chairs. Gunther and I sat down at one end of the table, but Eddie was still standing. He was about to ask Cassius about his helicopter plans but was more interested in the ledger's contents. He finally sat down next to me as Gunther set the log on the table.

The satyr opened the ledger's first page, a centuries-old piece of animal skin still in pristine condition. Carefully written script marked the center of the age-old page. The first line read: seven firestones valued at 10 conch shells each. In the same handwriting was a date going back several centuries.

"Conch shells?" Eddie asked, surprised.

"When the queendom was founded five thousand years ago, seashells were the currency at the time," Gunther explained. "Each shell held a monetary value. Sand dollars were worth one dollar, mussels worth five dollars, ten dollars for angel wings, clamshells worth twenty dollars; wentletrap shells fifty dollars, cowrie shells 100 dollars, argonauts 1,000 dollars, and conch shells 10,000 dollars."

He reached into his pocket and placed some silver coins on the table. The coins had pictures of various queens through the ages on one side and seashells on the reverse. A nod to Peregrin's past. He placed the change back in his pocket and turned to the next page.

This page was made out of papyrus and the words: seven firestones valued at 10,000 druci each at time of treatment. I looked at the date. "Hey, some pages seem to be missing," I said.

"Actually, no," Gunther said. "Every five hundred years, Hiram takes the seven firestones to a star in his galaxy where they undergo a mixture of heat and radiation treatment. When they come back, their values increase by 100 percent."

"Holy cow!" Eddie said as he did a quick calculation in his head. "That's a lot of money!"

"Well, Peregrin has been in existence for almost 5,000 years."

I remembered reading about heat treatments on gemstones. "I thought heat treatments are only used if the gems need more clarity and color, and heat treatments are supposed to be permanent," I remarked.

"That is true for ordinary gemstones, but firestones are different," Gunter explained. "Because they are not from earth, the firestones' colors and clarity faded over time. By the time five hundred years go by, the stones become completely colorless."

"The treatments are like a gem upgrade, increasing their value every time," Eddie said.

"Exactly," the satyr said. "The ledger is documentation of every treatment."

I turned to the last page. An actual ledger page with a three-hole punch on its edge. It read, "Seven firestones valued at 100 trillion dollars each at the time of treatment." It was signed by Queen Melissa.

Gunther saw me looking at the name. "Your grandmother," he said to me. "She and King Mark died during the Demon Wars." A faraway look briefly appeared in the satyr's eyes.

I nodded but said nothing. The Demon Wars was obviously still a painful subject for him, and I decided to steer the topic in another direction. "What I don't get is why Hiram would steal the firestones. If he actually stole them."

"That's what doesn't make sense," Eddie said. "I don't know this Hiram guy, but why would he suddenly change his loyalty to the crown?"

"And another thing, why put the freshly treated firestones back in the vault only to steal them later?" I said. "It would have made much more sense to never return with the firestones. That's how a lot of people steal library books. They check them out and never return them."

"That's why I believe he was framed," the satyr replied.

"His image was caught on the security camera." He grimaced at the evidence pointing to the prime minister. "Something is wrong. Hiram has never tried to harm the queen in all of Peregrin's history. He gave his word to never harm the queen. A pamola is compelled to keep his word."

"What happens if they don't?"

"They are banished forever from this planet."

"Let's get back to Hiram's strange behavior. Why change now?" Eddie asked

A smile crossed my face as a brilliant idea came to me. "What if someone was posing as Hiram?"

"Ah, crap!" Eddie moaned. "Not another doppelganger!"

"Maybe not," I countered. "What if it was another pamola? Like a relative of Hiram's who had a grudge against him? Gunther, would you like to come with us? You might have insight on what's going on."

The satyr was flabbergasted. Apparently, he wasn't used to the royals treating him as one of their own. "Of course. Whatever I can do to help."

Eddie leaned forward. "We need some sort of strategy."

I nodded. "I was thinking the same thing. I don't want to give away our suspicions."

"What about hand signals?" Gunther suggested.

"That would work," I replied.

"No," Eddie said, "hand signals can be easily read. Believe me, I've got twenty years of working in intelligence to prove it. A slight nod if it's Hiram or a shake of the head if it's not would be sufficient. "

"I can do that," Gunther said confidently.

"Your Majesties?" Cassius's voice boomed over the intercom. "We've arrived at the top of the mountain, but there's a fierce wind storm out there."

I looked around for the intercom button. The big silver button sat in the middle of the table. I got up and leaned over to press the button. "Is it safe to teleport us, Cassius?" I asked.

"I think so. But once you're on the ground, the Monte Carlo will have to get away from the wind storm."

"Okay. That'll be fine. We'll need three teleportation spheres. Just make sure you can do it safely."

"Will do, your Majesty. Signing off," the captain said.

I nearly toppled over as the airship lurched violently to the right. I managed to sit back in my seat and grabbed the edge of the table before my chair rolled away on its casters.

"Your Majesties, Gunther, the wind storm's getting worse. I'm sending the teleportation spheres right now. Get ready."

Moments later, the spheres flickered into existence. We quickly touched them and vanished out of the airship. As our molecules flew through time and space, I thought I heard an unfamiliar voice call for help. When we finally dematerialized, I was disoriented and a little nauseous. I felt myself start to topple backward when both Gunther and Eddie caught my arms.

"You all right, your Majesty?" Gunther asked.

"Yeah, I'm fine," I said, glancing over my shoulder. Only inches behind me was a 16,000-foot sheer drop off Mount Hottah into the foggy abyss. "Sorry about that. I wasn't paying attention. Teleportation on an empty stomach makes me a little queasy." The last part was a partial, white lie. I couldn't tell if I was actually sick or had another vision during the teleportation process. I glanced over at Eddie, who shot me a skeptical look.

I looked around for the first time and noticed how quiet it

was. A songbird trilled a melody on a nearby branch. The air was utterly still under a purple twilight sky. About a hundred feet ahead of us was the entrance to a large cave.

Eddie pressed the commlink and spoke, "Cassius, can you hear us?"

My vampire hearing picked up on the captain's crackling voice. "Just barely, sire! The winds are picking up here."

"Really?" Eddie asked. "There's no wind here."

"Guys," I said to Eddie and Gunther, "we need to get into that cave immediately, or things are going to get ugly. I'm 99% percent sure we're in the eye of the hurricane."

Eddie nodded in agreement. He spoke to Cassius. "Okay, we'll let you know when we need to be teleported back to the *Monte Carlo.* Signing off." He looked at me. "Okay, let's go!" We sprinted to the mouth of the cave just as hurricane-force winds began whipping around the mountaintop.

"Good call, your Majesty," Gunther said as we watched a tree branch fly across the entrance.

"Thanks," I said distractedly as I looked around me in awe. The cave walls glittered like a disco ball from thousands of glowing, bell-shaped flowers hanging from the ceiling.

"Glowbells!" I breathed in wonderment.

"Glowbells?" Eddie asked.

I pointed up the ceiling. "Bioluminescent flowers are grown only in caves. Each individual flower has a lifespan of fifty years. They have to grow in clusters to survive, which extends their life. Then that means—."

"When did you become a botanist?" Eddie interrupted.

"I read it in a book I was shelving when I worked at the library," I replied as I absentmindedly leaned against the wall. I jumped back in surprise. "The wall's pulsating! Yes! Yes! I've only read about this phenomenon!" I pointed to the wall like Vanya White showcasing a new car. "This is pneuma rock, a living, breathing organism. They always live near glowbells. They both feed off each other's energy."

"Okay, Shell. Thank you for the botany and geology lesson, but don't we have a job to do?"

I looked at my husband. "You're just jealous of my bookish knowledge."

"A little," he said with a smile. "That's why I married you."

"Come along, your Majesties," Gunther said to us. As he began to lead us deeper inside the mouth of the cave, the ceiling got taller. About a half a mile into the cave, we entered an 80-foot tall cavern. The glowbells were towering over us like stadium lighting. Loud snoring reverberated across the sparkling walls, making them shimmer like sun rays on a lake.

My ears and eyes followed the snoring to Hiram sitting on a large chair hewed from the mountain. His head rolled to one side. A long strain of drool dripped from the corner of his mouth. "Excuse me!" I shouted.

The pamola moaned something unintelligible before slowly waking up. He gave me a bleary-eyed stare. "Who are you?"

"Queen Shelly. You threw a temper tantrum at my coronation this morning."

"Oh, yeah. Well, I have a bone to pick with you. Your family accused me of stealing the firestones, which I would never do."

"To prove your point, you threw a temper tantrum?"

"Yes," Hiram said as he crossed his arms.

The prime minister was acting like a two-year-old who didn't get his way. I stole a sideways glance at Gunther, who slowly shook his head. We had a problem. If this guy was impersonating Hiram, then where was the real prime minister? I decided to play it close to the chest.

"Do you know who stole the firestones?"

"My brother, Laban, stole the firestones when I was bringing them back from their refinement process. I tried to pursue him, but he hid them in various traps."

"Um-uh," I said, not believing a word.

"Unfortunately, I can't get the firestones."

"You can't get the firestones?" Gunther shouted angrily. Out of the corner of my eye, I saw him ball his hands in tight fists and take a step forward. *Eddie*, I said mentally, *stop Gunther before he does something drastic.* I saw Eddie nod and place a hand on the satyr's shoulder, holding him back.

He leaned into Gunther's ear and whispered, "Let Queen Shelly handle him."

"Why not?" I asked the fake Hiram.

He gave a haughty sigh. "Because terrestrials are the only

ones who can retrieve the firestones."

"What's a terrestrial?'"

He pointed a finger at me. "You, the little people."

I looked around the large cavern. "Just to confirm, where is Laban?"

"I have him in a static electricity cage in the room behind me."

I stepped forward. "I should talk to Laban because he stole from the crown."

The pamola raised his hand to strike me, but Eddie stepped between us. He drew his scythe and pointed it at the fake Hiram. "Don't even think about it," he warned.

The snapping of electricity suddenly erupted above us. We all looked up into the ceiling as another emaciated, sickly-looking pamola trapped in a birdcage made entirely out of a yellow force field. "Laban!" he thundered angrily. "Let me out of here!"

The fake Hiram lazily snapped his fingers, and a volt of electricity zapped through the birdcage. The pamola was knocked back. He groaned in agonizing pain.

"Stop hurting him!" I shouted, but the injured pamola only received another electric shock. Anger began to build up in me at this display of bullying. "Okay, the game's up. By order of the queen, let Hiram go," I ordered.

"No," the imposter said loftily. "Why should I listen to an insignificant terrestrial like yourself? I am Hiram, the great—."

"Oh, come on!" Eddie said. "How stupid do you think we are? You're not Hiram. You've got him locked up in that force field."

He started slowly clapping his hands. "Well done, little terrestrials. You've used your almost nonexistent brains to deduce my clever plan. I, Laban, the greatest pamola, attempted to steal the firestones, but Hiram took them and hid them from me. I can't get to them because he placed them in places only terrestrials can enter."

An idea so brilliant came to me that I had to keep from grinning ear to ear. I was going to back the firestones, free Hiram, and give Laban a taste of his own medicine. *Eddie, I have a plan. Follow my lead*, I telepathically told my husband. I fell prostrate on the ground and began bowing and waving my hands dramatically before Laban. "Oh, great and wonderful Laban, we were wrong about you and your magnificent intellect. You are truly the smartest person in the universe."

I heard Gunther gasp at my melodramatic scene and was about to protest when Eddie grabbed his shoulder and yanked Gunther to his knees. My vampire hearing caught my husband hissing into the satyr's ear. "Play along."

I continued with my ego rubbing. "If our brains can handle it, my fellow terrestrials will find the firestones. We plead with you to release Hiram when you receive the firestones."

"You are willing to get into hazardous situations and possibly get killed to get your precious firestones. You're dumber than I thought."

You don't know me very well, do you? I thought, but I kept an insipid smile plastered to my face.

"Okay, we have a deal, but there are a couple of conditions," Laban said.

Of course, there is, I thought. "And what is that, O, Great One?"

"Only you and your Guardian must retrieve the firestones

and bring them to me one at a time."

Right, because if I die, the firestones' ownership will revert to the pamolas, I said telepathically to Eddie.

I highly doubt he'll free Hiram before he runs off with the firestones, Eddie replied.

There is no way in Hell I'm going to let that happen. I've gotten pretty good at keeping a straight face whenever I talked with Eddie telepathically, and this time was no exception. "I think our feeble minds think can handle that," I told Laban. I remembered Gunther's point about a pamola's word. That could work to our advantage. "Do you give your word to free Hiram once all the firestones are returned to you?" The ego massage was killing me, but I bravely maintained a bland expression on my face.

"I give you my word as a pamola, and because I tolerate you, I'll even stop the wind storm."

"Oh, thank you, oh wise, Laban. We all could learn greatly from you. May we go back and get some supplies before you send us off on our first quest?" Gunther, Eddie, and I scrambled to our feet and began to bow and back out of the cavern. Once we exited the cave, the windstorm had died off. Laban had kept part of his bargain. The *Monte Carlo* hovered above, and we had Cassius beam us into the conference room of the airship.

The second we arrived, Eddie asked me, "Care to share your great plan with the rest of the class?"

Gunther began his tirade. "Have you lost your mind, your Majesty?" he demanded of me. His hooves clicked on the thin-carpeted floor as he paced back and forth. "If you give Laban the firestones, you'll bankrupt the queendom!"

I held up a hand to silence him. "Gunther, I do have a plan," I told him.

He stopped pacing and looked at me. "That would be what?"

"I have devised a plan to get back the firestones, free Hiram, and hopefully get rid of Laban. We are going to con the con man." Then I went into more detail about my plan. Once I was finished, I looked at them. "So what do you think?"

"Absolutely brilliant, Shell," Eddie said with a huge grin. "How are we going to pull this off?"

It was Gunther's turn to grin. "I have something that might help with that."

"Good," I said to him, "you're in charge of that part of the plan. Put the results in your room safe on the Monte Carlo."

"I also suggest you talk to Dr. Charles Wandasen, the mainland's own eccentric inventor," Gunther said. "He might have some supplies to help you in your quests."

I looked over at Eddie. "Quest," I said, "I like the sound of that. I've always wanted to go on a quest."

"Sounds fun," Eddie agreed.

"How did it go?" Cassius asked as he came into the airship conference room.

"Good, I have a plan to get back the firestones, but I'll need you and your crew," I offered.

He nodded. "The Monte Carlo is at her Majesty's service."

Chapter Five:
Mad Scientists Give the Best Questing Items

Once we got back to the hanger, we dropped off Gunther at his house, telling him to meet us back at the Monte Carlo in two hours. I first conference-called all of my cabinet members to update them about the situation but gave them little detail about my plan. They were all in unsettled agreement. Once I had the cabinet's consent, Eddie and I decided to drive to Dr. Charles Wandasensen's place. "What do you think our first quest will be?" I asked Eddie.

"Probably somewhere incredibly dangerous and most likely to get us nearly killed."

"So just another typical adventure for us?"

"You got that right," Eddie said as he gave me a fist bump.

"By the way, Shell, fantastic plan. This is your best plan yet."

"Thanks, hon," I said. I looked down at the directions Gunther had given me. "Dr. Wandasen's mailbox number is 51."

Eddie pulled the car over. "We're here, I guess."

I looked up to see the short driveway ended at the base of a tall, thick tree. "Uh, where's his house or office or any building?" I looked around the property. Not a building in sight. "So, this guy lives in an empty lot?"

Eddie glanced at my directions. "Are you sure you wrote down the right directions?"

"Yeah, he lives on 51 Butterball Road." I reread the directions. "We have to knock four times on the tree. One short knock, one long knock, another short one—." I heard the driver side's door open and shut. I looked up to see my husband walking up the driveway. I scrambled out of the car and jogged up to the vampire. "What are you doing, Eddie?"

"It's not a real tree," Eddie replied. He pointed up to a cluster of leaves. "Those aren't real."

"You know this how?"

He smiled. "Watch and learn, babe. Duracell," he said. A

blue, marble-sized ball of energy appeared in his palm. He threw it at the leaves. The energy ball ricocheted off the leaves with a metal PING and came back at us at breakneck speed. We dropped to the ground, activated our shield bracelets, and placed them in front of our heads. The energy ball hit the grass a few inches in front of us, spraying dirt and grass onto the shields. I peeked out from my shield and looked at the ground. "Holy crap! Look at this, Eddie!"

He looked at the tiny, six-inch gouge in the grass. "Wow! Good thing we ducked. Imagine the damage it would've done to us!"

"Yeah, I don't think either one of us could have survived a six-inch hole to our heads. You know you could've thrown a clump of dirt or something other than an energy ball. In fact, if you had listened to me, I would've told you the tree is made of flexi-steel and fiberglass."

Eddie looked at me in surprise. "How did you know that? Did you have a vision?"

I waved a piece of paper in front of his face. "Does reading Gunther's instructions count as a vision?"

"Very funny," he replied.

I was about to answer when a peacock sitting on top of the tree suddenly stood up and splayed his tail feathers. A child-like cry erupted from its beak as floodlights burst from the "eyes" on the elongated feathers. More mechanical birds shouted out songs of alarms with their various voices. "Oh, this can't be good!"

"At least no one's shooting at us." Just as Eddie said that, an army of mechanical squirrels appeared from under the leaves and began chucking acorns at us. The little, brown missiles stung our arms and faces.

"You had to say it!" I looked at the directions before several acorns peppered the paper full of holes. "Once we give the secret knocks on the fake tree, Dr. Wandasen will let us in."

Eddie nodded. "Once there's a break in the missiles, we make a break for the tree." We saw our chance. "Now!" he said as we scrambled to our feet and raced to the trunk of the tree.

The door was so well hidden we would've missed it if it hadn't been for the rainbow mushroom doorknob. I gave the secret knocks, and a small window slid open.

A face appeared in the window. "Who is it?" a man demanded.

"The king and queen!" I shouted as the squirrels decided to change tactics and began dropping walnuts instead of acorns directly on our heads. I held up my shield before one of the walnuts could penetrate my skull.

"Are you sure?" the person behind the door asked. His grey eyes darted around anxiously.

"Yes, I'm sure!"

"They could have sent you to impersonate the king and queen."

"If you don't let us in, you'll be charged with regicide."

Several locks were turned and slid back before the door opened, and we were quickly ushered inside a room about as big as a shower stall and just as comfy.

We squished against a short, heavyset man. He wore a former white lab coat, now stained with various colors, over a dress shirt and a pair of slacks. But it was the pointy, wizard's hat sitting atop a shock of white Einstein hair sticking out in all directions that took our attention.

I squinted at it for a better look in the dim light. Is that tin foil? I mentally asked Eddie.

Eddie gave an imperceptible nod. Yeah, pretty elaborate design, though. Apparently, Gunther failed to mention this little quirk when telling us about Dr. Wandasen.

Well, Gunther did say he was eccentric. "Doctor Wandasen, I presume?" I asked.

"Yes, I am." He was about to shake our hands but instead pulled a roll of tin foil from his lab coat. "What's your favorite kind of hat, your Majesty?" he asked me.

"Uh, I don't really have one," I said hesitantly. "One of those bell-shaped hats that women wore in the twenties, I guess."

"And you, sire?"

"I've always been partial to tri-cornered pirate hats," Eddie said with just a hint of sarcasm.

Immediately, the man's big hands went to work. Within moments, he handed us two tin foil hats. "Put these on your heads," he ordered us. "It'll keep them from reading your mind."

"Who is 'them?'" I asked.

Dr. Wandasen's eyes traveled up to the ceiling. "The aliens," he whispered.

I looked up. "Are they in the ceiling?" I asked.

"Maybe. If you put on these hats, they can't hear your thoughts and use their mind control. Anyone who visits me must wear their hats."

I placed the hat on my head. "Well then, we wouldn't want any kind of alien mind control invading our heads." I shot Eddie a humor-him look.

"I really like pirate hats," my husband said as he put on his hat.

Dr. Wandasen smiled broadly. He reached over my shoulder and pressed a button with a down arrow. Instantly, the room began descending into the darkness. An LCD screen counted down the digital numbers to one. The doors opened into a small cramped laboratory no bigger than a studio apartment. Six tables were filled with organized clutter of half-finished inventions. At the end of the room was one of those old-fashioned computers with a large screen in its middle.

"Follow me, your Majesties." Dr. Wandasen led us to one

of the cluttered tables. "Mr. Hornicus told me you were going on some quests, and I have the perfect equipment." He grabbed two small items from the table and handed them to Eddie and me, "I present to you: the Tomlinson."

I looked at the object in my hands. "Pardon my skepticism, but how is an umbrella going to be useful?"

"This is no ordinary umbrella. It's a teleportation umbrella. Once you open up the canopy, two buttons will appear right above the handle. The bottom one opens and closes the umbrella, and the top one will transport you anywhere you want to go. All you have to do is press the button and say, 'Take me to (wherever you want to go) in foo mickins."

Eddie and I exchanged confused looks. "Did you just say, 'foo mickins?'" my husband asked. "I'm fairly certain that's not even a real phrase."

"Actually, it's a very ancient phrase, meaning 'in a few moments,'" Dr. Wandasen said in a rather unconvincing tone. He went to another table and grabbed a black fanny pack, which should have belonged in the 1980s. "I have something else for your journey." He began tossing random objects into the bag. No matter how many things he put in, the bag never got bigger. "I call it the 'infinity bag.'"" After emptying it, he handed the fanny pack to Eddie. "Here you go, sire."

Eddie promptly gave the fanny pack to me. "Since the queen is primarily responsible for the retrieval of the firestones, I think she should be the one in charge of the fanny pack."

I shot a subtle but very annoyed look at my husband. I reluctantly put the fanny pack around my waist. I tried to read his mind, but the hats blocked my telepathy. These tin foil hats actually worked. Who knew?

I wandered over to the end of the workshop and looked at the large computer screen where a large contraption hovered over the main island. "What's this?"

Dr. Wandasen smiled widely. "Ah, my most successful invention yet."

Eddie and I exchanged wary glances. If this contraption was his most successful, why did he just provide us with crappy, second-rate inventions that may or may not work? I decided to the best approach to my question would be a diplomatic one. "Tell us about it. Can we take it with us?"

"Absolutely not! The Palmer machine is the main island's food source."

"What do you mean?"

"This machine replicates giant food. This helps feed the entire island every week."

"By raining food?"

"Yes."

"Isn't that dangerous?" Eddie asked. "What if a giant doughnut squashes several people?"

"Not at all, sire," Dr. Wandasen replied. "The floating food only comes at certain times on Sundays in delegated areas, so there is no danger."

"Okay," I said. "I would like to see that someday."

"Certainly, the next drop is on the school's football field at 4 am next Sunday morning."

"Wow, that's a little early," I replied, "but not bad for a one time deal." I stole a glance at Eddie, who looked relieved to know we wouldn't be getting up that early regularly.

"Is there anything else you think we might need, doctor?" I asked.

"Nothing else, your Majesty."

"Thank you for your help. I'm sure these tools will come in handy," I said. Eddie and I started to leave when the doctor called us back.

"I would like your hats back, please. You can use them whenever you come to visit." We gave back the tin foil hats and left his laboratory.

By the time we arrived back at the castle, both our stomachs were growling with hunger. The moment we got into the foyer, Rupert greeted us. "How was your visit to Hiram's?" he asked.

"Somewhat productive. We kind of have to go on a few quests."

"Really?" Rupert was surprised.

"Long story, but the short end of it is pretty simple. Once we retrieve the lost firestones, we will rescue the prime minister," I said as Eddie and I walked to our private elevator.

"Well, you certainly can't go anywhere without a meal. Now, the cook has prepared you a full lunch in the dining hall."

What a lunch it was! Eddie and I filled up on roasted eggplant, mashed potatoes with peas, chicken breast stuffed with broccoli and cheese, and Caesar salads. For dessert, we had fresh strawberry pie with ice cream. After eating, we went up to our suite, changed into jeans, T-shirts, and sneakers. Eddie grabbed a backpack, and we packed it with two headlamps, a first-aid kit, and several water bottles, all of which we gathered from various rooms and people in the castle. We hurried back to the Monte Carlo.

Gunther greeted us when Eddie and I arrived aboard the airship. "I have that object I told you about, your Majesty." He took us to his room and demonstrated its ability.

"Perfect," I said with a grin. I looked at Eddie. "Let's go get us some firestones."

Chapter Six:
Indiana Jones, We Ain't

Eddie and I stood at the bottom of Mount Demise, staring at the flint rock face. "So, where exactly is this hidden door?" Eddie asked.

"Somewhere we can't find it. Which is the very definition of hidden," I replied as I felt along the wall. "Hiram said there is a button with fleur-de-lis engraved on it. When pressed, it will open up the door." I crouched down and brushed away some weeds along the bottom. A light suddenly shone in my eyes. "Are you going to help look or play with the flashlight?" I asked.

"Sorry," Eddie answered. He searched the wall for a few seconds. Then he shouted, "Found it!"

I got up and stood beside him. "Where is it?"

"Up there."

I followed Eddie's flashlight beam one hundred feet above

us. I placed my hands on my hips. "Well, that's convenient. How are we going to open it?"

Eddie grinned. "Allow me. Duracell!" A medium-sized, blue sphere of energy appeared in the palm of his hand. He threw at the engraving but missed it by at least ten feet.

"Now I can see why you weren't the pitcher for Zephyr's baseball team."

"Oh, you can do better?"

"Watch this," I said with a grin. I pulled out my crossbow pistol and aimed it at the button. The arrow flew straight and true, hitting the rock knob with a soft THUNK. A loud, grinding noise shook the ground we stood on as a door about three-and-half feet tall and four feet wide opened up. Eddie and I stared in disbelief at the silliness of the door's placement. "That's the door?" I asked.

"Shouldn't it be taller as the doorknob is one hundred feet above it?" Eddie mused.

"Well, Hiram did say to keep on our toes," I said. I walked up to the opening, got down on my hands and knees, and began crawling into the mountain. "You coming, hon?"

"Of course." Eddie came crawling after me.

The door was only a few feet deep, and both of us stood up as we glanced around at our surroundings. Dust fell like snowflakes from the cathedral-high ceiling in the dark, ancient room hewed from the inside of the mountain. Three giant doorways led into blackness. "Really? A tiny door to a giant room? Who designed this place?" I ranted between coughing fits.

Eddie slid off his backpack and took out the headlamps. He tossed one to me before putting his own on. "Done with your ranting?" he asked, flicking on the light.

"For now," I said. I turned on my headlamp and pulled out the instructions Hiram had given me. "Okay, to navigate these catacombs, we need to take the middle doorway to the Bridge of Expiration, then take the next left to the Room of Destruction, and take a right through a hallway. The firestone will be in the Room of Happiness."

"Let's go through the non-scary, dark doorway," Eddie said as he slipped the backpack onto his shoulders. We walked through the correct entrance into a short hallway with a dull, glowing light at the end. "Wow!" my husband said. "Is it me, or is it getting hot in here?"

Sweat began to drip into my eyes. "Holy cow! You're right! It's like a sauna in here. We should have one of these in our suite."

"A dark hallway?"

"No, a sauna."

"I think there's one in the pool room."

I sighed. "What I would give to take a dip in our infinity pool?"

We reached the end of the hallway and were greeted by a blast of hot air. "Well, we know where the heat's coming from," Eddie said as we glanced over the edge of a large, deep ravine. At its bottom ran a thick line of bubbling lava.

I pointed to a rickety-looking rope bridge. "That must be the Bridge of Expiration." I grimaced at the fraying ropes, barely holding them together. "I'm no civil engineer, but that bridge doesn't seem even remotely safe."

"I agree," Eddie said. "It's about forty feet across. There is no way either one of us can jump it. At least, the fall won't kill us.”

“No, that will be the boiling lava’s job.”

“We should go back to the Monte Carlo and see if there’s anything aboard that can help,” Eddie suggested. A rumbling came from behind us. Dust and small rocks started falling. Eddie pulled me to him and shouted, “Citadel!” A green force field surrounded us as I waited for the entire mountain to come crashing down. But that’s not what happened. A stone door slid down into the doorway we had just walked through, permanently blocking our way to the entrance.

I looked at my husband, who dissipated his force field when the coast was clear. “You were saying?”

“We probably should cross the bridge if we want to get out of here,” Eddie said as he walked to the bridge. He looked at it. “I’ll go first,” he said as he took a tentative step on the boards. “So far, so good.” He glanced over his shoulder. “Come on, but take it slow.”

The boards creaked under our feet as we slowly made our way across the ravine. I grabbed the ropes for support and could feel them disintegrating under my touch. “I think we should report this unsafe bridge to somebody."

"And who would that be?" Eddie asked.

"I don't know. The bridge builders' guild?"

"Peregrin has guilds?"

"We should."

My husband took another step, and the boards under his feet crumbled. He gave a shout of surprise. If it hadn't been for the ropes he was holding, he would've followed the boards' demise into the river of lava.

"Eddie!" I shouted. My heart thumped in my chest. "Hang on. I'm coming." My legs suddenly felt like wet pasta as the bridge swayed wildly. I hurried to him. Quickly accessing the situation, I realized I needed to get on the other side of the hole. After carefully stepping over the large hole, I got on my stomach and stretched out my hand to him. "Eddie, grab on!"

He reached out and grasped my wrist with his free hand. "Pull me up!" He let go of the rope and took my other hand with a sharp cry of pain.

I scrambled to my feet, and I pulled him back on the bridge using all of my vampiric strength. "Go! Go! Go!" I shouted as I felt more boards start to give way underneath us. We raced the rest of the way to the other side, gripping each other's hands. The moment we stepped onto solid ground, the bridge collapsed behind us, plummeting into the ravine. We leaned against the wall and sank to the rock floor. I placed my head against Eddie's shoulder.

He winced in pain. "I did something to my shoulder when I fell."

"Could it be dislocated?" I asked.

"Maybe. I'll just pop it back into place." Grimacing, he lifted his injured arm over his head and rotated his shoulder a couple of times before it popped back into place.

"Ooh, that looks painful, hon."

"Not too bad. I've done it before." He looked at me with admiration before giving me a passionate kiss. "I bet not many guys can say that their wives have saved them from a falling bridge."

"Those are some very unlucky guys."

Eddie got two bottles of water out of his backpack, and we drank about half of the bottles. The combined heat from the lava river and the excursion of the rescue had made us very parched.

After a few moments of rest, we got up and walked through another doorway. "I just hope this door doesn't close on us like all the others," I said, glancing over my shoulder. Nothing happened. The room was large and tall. Rows upon rows of holes the size of manhole covers lined the walls. I stopped and examined one of the cavities. It was completely dark inside. I was about to stick my head in the hole to investigate further when I heard the sound of mental swiftly scraping against stone. "Get down!" I shouted to Eddie. We both dropped to the ground as a giant metal spike raced out of its hidey-hole. It slammed into the opposite wall. Several more spikes began to shoot out from the holes in the wall.

"Shelly, I think you triggered something," Eddie said.

"Yes, I realize that now. Note to self: Don't stick head in mysterious holes." I looked around at the spikes attempting to impale us. The lowest rows of spikes were only about three feet from the ground. The only way we could make it across to the end of the room was to army-crawl our way to the doorway. I was about to tell Eddie my slip-shod plan when something terrible

began to happen. Another hidden door began slowly cutting off

our exit. "How good are you at army crawling?" I asked my

husband.

"I don't know. I've never thought about it before."

"I think now would be a good time to think about it."

Apparently, vampires are excellent army-crawlers. We can crawl

at astonishing speeds. We raced towards the door as it slowly

closed ahead of us. It was only two feet from trapping us with the

spike.

"Shelly, we need to shape-shift, or we won't make it!"

Eddie said. He immediately turned himself into a cloud of green

mist and darted under the door.

I swallowed hard and concentrated. In my short time as a

vampire, I had only shape-shifted once before. That was just a

fluke. Were there magic words I had to say? Think, Shelly, think.

I let my mind drift back to the moment I morphed. I thought about

the power, agility, and furiousness to protect myself and those

around me had brought me. The air shimmered around me.

Brown dust particles turned into specks of black and gold as my clothes and body melded in the sleek, powerful physique of a black panther. I let out a primal scream as I bounded towards the door, leaping over the deadly spikes. With the grace of a cat, I slid effortlessly under the door. As I changed back, the door slammed shut behind me.

Eddie looked at me with a sly grin. "Is it wrong for me to say that whenever you change into a black panther, I get a little turned on?"

"At this particular moment, yes." I looked around. We had landed in another hallway with two doorways. We took the one to the left and would have killed ourselves if the lights on our headlamps hadn't shown us the sudden drop-off into oblivion.

We took the correct hallway and stood at the entrance of a large, almost empty room. The only item in the room was a stone pedestal with a softball-sized yellow gem. "Not really a safe place to store the firestone," I mused as I looked around, searching the room for any more booby-traps. No hidden spikes, no broken rope bridges. I took a step inside. Nothing happened. "Well, I'm going for it." I was about to take another step when I heard a click-click like someone was trying on a gas stove burner.

Eddie yanked me back just in time. A complex system of fire geysers began sprouting at various intervals. The flames disappeared into thousands of slits in the floor. The slits formed several circles, one inside each other. There was about a two-foot space between each ring. The pedestal stood in the very middle of the group of rings. He glanced at me. "Babe, you're incredibility hot, but I would prefer you not extra-crispy."

"My love continually burns for you,"

"Ooh, good pun. You're on fire."

"I know. You can't extinguish my wittiness." I looked at the fire fountains, trying to figure out the patterns. "Okay, let's get back to our hot problems." I couldn't resist sliding in another pun.

Eddie studied the flames as they danced up and down in intricate patterns for a few minutes. An idea came to him. "Every five seconds, the fire geysers will go off."

"Okay," I replied. I readied myself to run. "Time me."

Eddie nodded as he looked at me with concern in his striking green eyes. "Be careful," he said. "We vampires aren't fireproof."

I kissed him quickly. "Don't worry, I'll be careful," I promised.

Eddie glanced at his watch. "Go!" he said.

I sprinted only a couple of feet when Eddie told me to stop. I did, right before a six-foot geyser of fire erupted from the wall and disappeared back into the slits. I let out a breath I didn't know I was holding. I had no time to think about it because Eddie told me to go. I raced forward another couple of feet before Eddie shouted, "Stop!" This fiery version of Red Light, Green Light went on for another few minutes, but soon I reached the pedestal.

The firestone was gorgeous up close. The clear stone's yellow color glinted in the fire fountains. The middle of the gem was a darker yellow in the shape of a flame. I picked up the stone, surprised at how heavy it was, about two pounds. I unzipped the infinity fanny pack and dropped the firestone inside. "Got it," I said to Eddie.

"Great," Eddie replied. "Ready?"

"Yep."

He checked his watch. "Go!"

I had just started sprinting when a wave of dizziness coupled with nausea swept over me. I fell to my knees, barely feeling the fire as it grazed my palms. The world around me started to fade.

Hiram hands Queen Aquila a gift basket. Seven brightly colored gemstones shimmer through the clear cellophane. "Thank you for taking care of me, your Majesty."

"It was a pleasure," she replies as she exchanges a large bouquet of dandelions, Queen Anne's lace, thistle, ragweed, goldenrod, buttercups, nightshade, creeping Charlie, and clovers. Stuck in the middle of the flowers was a Get Well Soon balloon on a stick.

A horrified look appears on her face as Laban appears behind Hiram. She can barely give a warning shout before Hiram crumples to the ground from a huge, open gash in his side, golden blood gushing onto the floor. My ancestor fades out of existence.

A malicious grin spreads easily across Laban's face as he tosses the fiery, bronze sword carelessly to the side. "Just like old times, Hiram?" he sneers as he steps over his brother. He tries to grab the gift basket, but it vanishes before his eyes. He kicks Hiram in the side and demands to know the location of the gift basket.

"They are hidden in places where no celestial beings can tread," Hiram said between gasps of pain.

"You will change your mind and give me access to the locations, or you will die a slow, agonizing death." He grabs Hiram roughly by his antlers and drags him into the darkness.

"Not the best time to have a vision, Shell," I heard Eddie say as I slowly came back to reality. My husband was by my side, his arms wrapped around me. One of his force fields encased us as the fiery fountains spurted around us. He glanced at my hands. "You've got some nasty burns there."

I glanced down at my slowly healing hands. "I must have fallen forward. How did you know I had a vision?"

"Your eyes cloud over when you have one."

"Really?"

He nodded. "I put a force field around you to keep you

safe until I got over here."

"How long was I out?"

"Ten minutes or so."

"Wow, the vision seemed a lot shorter." I closed my hands into fists and grimaced in pain. "Let's try out those Tomlinson umbrellas and get out of here."

Eddie took out one of the umbrellas and opened the large canopy after taking down the force field. He wrapped his free arm around my waist and said, "Take us to the Monte Carlo in foo mickins!" We disappeared into a puff of black smoke.

Have you ever been driving on an icy road and went into an unstoppable skid? That was exactly how our first experience with the Tomlinson umbrella was like. When we came back out of time and space, we were going about 30 mph at the least. Eddie's quick thinking of closing the umbrella and tossing it out of the way most likely prevented anyone from getting impaled. We rolled head over heels into some swivel chairs, scattering the occupants and the chairs all over the airship bridge.

Cassius and his first mate, the gorilla, Moses Heston, ran

to us. "Are you all right, your Majesties?" the captain asked as he helped me to my feet.

"Yeah, we're fine." I turned to Eddie. "It seems that Dr. Wandasen forgot to give us some important instructions about these umbrellas."

"Ya think?" my husband asked as he scooped up the umbrella and placed it securely back in the backpack. "How're your hands?" he asked me.

I held up my palms. "All healed with my vampiric powers," I said with a grin.

"Your Majesty," Cassius said, "Gunther wanted to let you know he is waiting for you in his room."

"Thank you, Cassius," I said. Eddie and I left the bridge, walked to Gunther's room, and knocked.

The satyr opened the door and let us in. "Were you successful in your quest, your Majesty?" he asked me.

"Very much so," I said as I reached into the infinity fanny pack and pulled out the firestone. "Here you go."

His eyes widen in awe as he held the firestone in his hands. "I never thought I would see the firestones again in my lifetime," he murmured. "This is truly amazing." He looked at me with tears in his eyes. "You are doing a great thing for Peregrin."

"So are you, Gunther."

He smiled. "I'll have the firestone ready for you within ten minutes."

Eddie and I went back to our room and sat back on the bed to wait for Gunther. My husband leaned back against the pillows and placed his hands behind his head. "So, what was your vision about?" he asked.

"Weird," I said. I describe it to Eddie. "What do you think?"

"That Laban was probably responsible for injuring Hiram the first and second time."

"True, but about what the bouquet of weeds?"

"Someone can't tell a weed from a flower?"

I narrowed my eyes at him. "Would it kill you to be serious for once?

"Probably."

There was a knock on our door. "Come in!" I shouted.

Gunther opened the door and stepped inside. He handed

me the firestone. "All set, your Majesty."

I looked at the stone and grinned. "Oh, this is perfect." I put it back in my fanny pack. I pressed the intercom button on the phone by our bed. "Cassius, can you take us back to Mount Hottah?"

Chapter Seven:
We Come Between a Roc And a Hard Place.

The coordinates Hiram gave us for our second quest led us to the top of Mount Demise instead of the bottom. We surveyed the high slopes of the mountaintop before us. I glanced at the GPS on Eddie's phone screen. "Please tell me we're close."

"Unfortunately, no. We've got about a mile-long hike."

"Lovely," I muttered. We began traipsing uphill to our final destination. I started thinking about my vision. For the most part, it was very easy to decipher. Laban wanted the firestones for whatever nefarious purpose he was concocting. Most likely take over the world or whatever evil villains did these days. "Do you

have any ideas why Laban is so desperate to take the firestones,
Eddie?" I asked as we stopped for a short break.

Eddie leaned against a rock, took out a bottle of water
from his backpack, and took a swig before handing it to me.
"Maybe the firestones can be ground up and snorted."

I took a drink and put the bottle away. "As in drug use?"

"Sure, why not?"

"Because gemstones aren't used in the drug-making
process."

"Maybe not here on earth, but maybe wherever Hiram and
Laban come from, they are used for both legal and illegal drug
use."

"As crazy as that sounds, it makes sense. Laban does act
like an addict. Okay, that solves one problem. What about the
bouquet of weeds? That must have some sort of significance."

Eddie shrugged as we started our trek again. "Probably,"
he replied as we descended a short, rocky hill. He checked his
phone, not paying attention to his surroundings. "According to
the GPS—by the way, it's a miracle I'm getting a strong

signal—the firestone should be at the bottom of this hill."

"Well, this could be a slight problem." I tapped Eddie's arm to get his attention. When he looked up, I pointed to a very tall wall of bramble, at least twenty-five-feet high. Trees as thick as cars were piled methodically. Most of them had been yanked out from the roots. I scanned the walls for any sign of the gemstone.

"The firestone must be beyond this wall," Eddie said as he put away his phone. "Over or under?"

"Over is probably the fastest way." We began to scale the barrier. We had only gotten a few feet up when my fingers brushed against something cold and hard. "Whoa!" I said in surprise.

Eddie was right above me. He stopped and turned his head towards me. "You okay?"

"Yeah, but I just touched metal." I inspected what I had touched. It wasn't even wood, but the steel track of a roller coaster.

"Oh, good!" Eddie said. "I thought I was hallucinating when I touched a part of a cell tower."

"What is a part of a cell tower and a roller coaster track doing on top of a mountain?" I asked as we continued to climb.

"Beats me," my husband replied. As we scaled the barrier, we encountered a few cables from suspension bridges, a few steel ship masts, and a few train engines. I tried to figure out how these man-made things got to the mountaintop.

By the time we reached the top, I had found out. The circumference of the wall was as big as a football field and bowl-shaped. The interior was littered with rainbow-colored dragon eggs of all sizes. "It's a nest! But definitely not a dragon's," I said

Eddie nodded. "Hopefully, the nest has long been abandoned. Ready for the climb down?"

"Definitely!" We climbed down into the giant nest and began to scour around for the firestone. About half an hour into the search, I felt something brush up against my leg. I looked down to see a furry, serpentine creature the size of a house cat rubbing against me. It was a catnip dragon. This particular cat-dragon hybrid had a mated, thin layer of fur covering his blue scales.

"Where did you come from?" I asked as I squatted down to pet him. With a flutter of his green butterfly wings, he glided up to me and landed on my shoulder. He happily licked my face as his little green whiskers tickled my face. The black pet id tag dangled from a red collar read the name: Alonzo.

As I looked around for any sign of his owners, the dragon jumped off my shoulder and ran into the remains of a single prop plane crammed into the nest's structure. The steel propeller had been torn off by something with giant talons or claws. I could still see the gashes imbibed in the nose of the plane.

Alonzo entered the cockpit and began pawing and meowing at the skeletal remains of the dwarf pilot slumped over in his seat. Bits of glass were jammed into the hairline fracture on the white skull. He must have died from a major concussion during the crash.

I picked up the little dragon and scratched him behind his cat ears thoughtfully. "So, Alonzo, how did you and your owner end up here?"

He purred happily in response as he nuzzled his head into my shoulder.

"Found it!" Eddie shouted from the other side of the nest. I looked up to see him jumping down from the deck of a mangled sailboat. He was lazily tossing bright orange firestone back and forth. When he got closer, his eyes immediately went to the little dragon in my hands. "What are you holding?"

I nearly shoved the dragon in his face. "Say hello to Alonzo, Eddie." I mimicked Alonzo waving his paw at my husband.

"No, and we're not keeping him."

"Why not? He's so cute."

"He probably already has an owner."

"Not anymore." I jerked my thumb over to the plane.

Eddie took one look at the cockpit. "No way! I know this guy!" He began to circle the plane.

"You do?"

"Not personally. This is Randolph Grimm's plane."

"Who?"

Eddie saw the blank expression on my face. "Reckless Randolph, the daredevil, multi-billionaire?"

"Never heard of him."

"According to a recent article in *Cart Before the Horse* mechanical magazine, he would do crazy, stupid stunts, like hanging from a flying plane, going down a waterfall in a barrel, and even driving a motorcycle on a tightrope across two skyscrapers. Most of the time, he was completely baked."

"So, you looked up to a stoner?"

"No, the surprisingly long life of Reckless Randolph was more of a morbid fascination for me."

"Like a train wreck!"

Eddie nodded. "Exactly."

"Was this idiot married?"

"She divorced him and completely cleaned out his bank account. The only thing he got was his private plane and one of the catnip dragons she bred. Reckless Randolph vanished, saying he was going to pull off his biggest, craziest stunt ever."

I held out the little dragon for Eddie to observe. "Here's something to remember him by."

My husband sighed as he continued to toss the firestone to and from his hands. He had given up trying to convince me not to abandon Alonzo. "Fine, we'll take home him with us."

I gave my husband a quick kiss on the cheek. "He'll grow on you," I assured him. "Let's put away the firestone." I set Alonzo down on the ground. Eddie tossed me the gemstone, and I put it away in my infinity fanny pack. That's when I noticed something missing. "Where's the backpack?"

Eddie threw his thumb over his shoulder. "I left it by that dilapidated sailboat. I took it off to search the wreckage."

"Why?"

"I didn't want it to get caught on something while I crawled through the wreckage."

"You do realize our only method of getting out of here is in your backpack?"

"I am well aware of it," Eddie replied.

I looked at him and then at the backpack, which was on the other side of the nest, before sighing. "I just hope whatever lives here isn't coming back anytime soon."

"Don't worry. The nest was probably abandoned a long time ago. Plus, it'll only take us a few minutes to get the backpack."

I realized the need to debate was useless at this point as

we walked back to the sailboat. I took another good look around the nest and noticed a big pile of animal bones I had mistaken for white birch trees for the first time. I stopped to get a closer look. "Eddie, what type of bones are those?" I asked as I ducked under a row of gleaming white, curved bones.

My husband stopped and inspected the cartilage. "Whale rib cage, maybe?"

"Whoa!" I breathed in astonishment. "Can dragons carry off an entire whale?"

"I don't think so. The largest dragon is about as big as two horses."

I looked at the skeletal remains, from the skull to the tail. "What can carry an entire whale to a mountain top?"

The body of a fire-breathing elephant answered my question when it dropped from the sky to the floor a few yards from where we were standing. We looked to see a vast shadow circling overhead and blocking half the sky. As it came into view, I could make out the outline of a giant bird the size of a Boeing airplane beginning its descent into the nest. "What is that?"

"It's a roc," Eddie replied as he pulled me back into the

shadows of the whale skeleton.

"That is not a rock," I said. I pointed to the granite floor of the nest. "That is a rock."

"R-o-c, Shelly, not r-o-c-k."

"Oh," I said in realization. I sat on the floor. We watched the giant bird land and pick apart the dead elephant. I turned away before my stomach started a rebellion.

Eddie sat next to me and looked at me with anticipation. "So, what's the plan?"

This was a pretty standard question in our relationship. I always seemed to come up with crazy plans to get us out of any sticky situations. I was fresh out of ideas this time, but when I looked into the vampire's eyes, I just couldn't disappoint him. "You know the saying: Patience is a virtue. Virtue is a grace. Well, here's my plan: We are going to sit here and wait. And wait. And wait. And wait."

Eddie made a rolling motion with his hand. "And?"

"We wait some more until the roc leaves," I concluded.

"That's a terrible plan."

"Okay, smartypants, do you have a better plan?"

"No."

"Crap." I let out a sigh of defeat. Alonzo wriggled loose and darted towards the giant bird. "Get back here," I hissed at him. I scrambled to my feet. I was torn between not wanting the adorable guy to become birdseed and not giving away our hiding place.

The catnip dragon promptly ignored me and let out a shrill hiss at the roc. The bird stopped eating and turned its head to inspect the little disruption. It ruffled its black and white feathers and let out a deafening yak-yak-yak. Alonzo arched his back as the skin around his neck frilled around his head. This little act of bravery or stupidity (I wasn't sure which) infuriated the roc. It turned around and grabbed at the dragon with his sharp, black beak. Alonzo wasn't going to make it.

"Citadel!" Eddie said as we scrambled to our feet. He summoned a green force field and threw it around Alonzo. "Okay, I have a plan."

"Anything's better than doing nothing."

"You're not going to like my plan."

"What is it?"

"Run." With me following on his heels, he raced out of the skeleton towards Alonzo, dismantled the force field, and scooped him up. The roc tried to impale them with his beak, but the former wizard turned vampire hurled a ball of energy one-handed at the creature. Unfortunately, this line of defense caused my husband to stumble and fall on his rear. Alonzo escaped from him and made a beeline for the backpack. The roc didn't seem to care. It focused its black eyes on Eddie as it prepared to feast on a fresh vampire. He was right: I didn't like his plan.

Thank god, my love of obscure knowledge came to our rescue. My parents had a book on birds, and I realized this airplane-sized avian was essentially a giant magpie. I remembered how much magpies love shiny objects. This roc's nest was full of massive shiny things. I tapped the button underneath my shield bracelet and unleashed my metal shield, Truth. I let the light of the moon catch its shiny front and shone it into the roc's eyes.

Eddie scrambled to his feet with the bird distracted and activated his shield bracelet as he raced towards me. "Great plan, Shelly, but now it's going towards you."

"I am well aware of that, Eddie." I slowly led the bird back to the whale skeleton as a more realistic plan formed in my head. "Just get over here and help me with my plan."

Eddie was by my side in an instant. "Is this plan actually going to work?"

"I'm 80 percent sure it'll work."

"What is it?"

"We chuck the whale skull at the bird with just enough force to stun it."

"Got it." We deactivated our shields and hefted the already detached nineteen-foot long whale skull. If we weren't vampires, we would've struggled under its massive weight. "Ready?" he asked.

"Ready!" Combining our vampiric strength, we chucked the skull at the roc's head. Our makeshift projectile hit its target, and the bird wobbled on its legs before toppling to the ground with a loud WHUMP! A cloud of dust plumed in the comatose bird's wake.

We waited anxiously for a few moments to see if we had utterly incapacitated the giant magpie. The only movement was the feathered chest moving up and down. "Okay," Eddie decided, "let's get out of here."

"Now that's a great plan."

We ran to the backpack, where Alonzo was patiently waiting for us. I gathered him up in my arms, where he began purring contentedly. Eddie got out the Tomlinsons and tossed one to me. We opened them up and said the magical words. Before we knew it, we were whisked away to the *Monte Carlo*.

Our entrance on the airship's bridge was precisely the same as the first time we used the teleportation devices. The one exception was me hip-checking Gunther upon entry. The satyr was sent careening into the steering wheel and nearly knocked Moses Heston, Cassius' first mate, off his feet. "Is anyone hurt?" I asked as we all pulled ourselves together.

There was a resounding no, except for a whimpering Alonzo. I looked at him and noticed one of his paws was hanging limply. The poor little guy got hurt during the melee. "Hey, Cassius, can your wife help our new friend?"

"I think so." The airship captain looked at the catnip

dragon. "It looks like he injured his foot and is malnourished. These dragons are domesticated. Wherever did you find him?"

"In a roc's nest."

The room fell silent at my announcement as everyone on the bridge gawked at Eddie and me. Apparently, not many people survive encounters with these giant birds. "But we got the firestone!" I said in a failed attempt to brush over the fact their new queen had nearly gotten herself killed twice so far.

"That's wonderful, your Majesty," Cassius replied hesitantly. He decided not to ask any more questions. "I'll call Delilah and let her know you're coming with the dragon."

"Thanks, Cassius," I said.

"Forget these quests. Using these umbrellas is going to be the death of us," Eddie remarked as he gathered up the Tomlinsons and put them in his backpack.

I nodded. "I think we need to have a talk with Doctor Wandasen before we use them again. Cassius, where's the best place to make a secure call?"

"Actually, your Majesty," Gunther interrupted, "I have a message from Dr. Wandasen regarding the umbrellas."

"A message?" I asked.

"He called me while you were out. Unfortunately, it's very vague. I better let you listen to it. My phone is in my room if you would follow me." As Eddie and I walked with the satyr, he said, "Not many people have escaped the clutches of a roc, your Majesty."

"I got that impression from the looks on your faces," I said.

"How did you escape?"

"We threw a skull at it," Eddie replied.

"Oh!" Gunther gave an impressed nod but asked no more. Once we reached his room, he retrieved his phone and played the voicemail for us.

"Mr. Hornicus, please inform the queen that the umbrellas I gave her and her Guardian may need to be adjusted to avoid injury in the landings. I recommend the green and red wires are switched from their connectors. Thank you." The recording ended. "I'm sorry, your Majesty, but that's it."

"Don't worry about it, Gunther," Eddie said. "I can fix them, no problem. I'll just need to borrow a few tools from the engine room. I'll meet you in the infirmary, Shelly."

"Okay," I said, giving Eddie a kiss. Once he had left, I handed my private secretary the firestone. "Gunther, can I have Dr. Wandasen's phone number?"

"You're worried about the king's tinkering?"

"No, Eddie will get the Tomilsons repaired. I'm just worried about Dr. Wandasen's instructions."

Gunther nodded as he handed me the eccentric scientist's phone number. "In my dealings with him, Dr. Wandasen tends to be very vague."

The infirmary was on the top level. Eddie met me just outside the door with a small toolkit in his hands. Delilah Winters, the ship's doctor, is a plump, smiling vampire in her four hundreds but doesn't look a day over forty. She looked up from prepping a small table with various medical equipment. "Come in, your Majesties." Her gray eyes looked at the injured Alonzo with concern. "What happened to you?" she asked him.

"I think he injured his paw when we accidentally crash-landed into the bridge," I said. "Will he be all right?"

"Set him on the table," the doctor said. She inspected his

paw by gently lifting it. This set off a shrill squawk of pain from the dragon.

I stroked his head, and he calmed down.

"I'll have to take an x-ray, but I think it might be broken." Delilah walked to the intercom phone and paged someone named Louise to the infirmary.

Moments later, a silverback gorilla in red scrubs came into the infirmary. "Yes, doctor?" she asked.

"This is Louise, the ship's nurse. Louise, this is Queen Shelly and King Eddie. Their catnip dragon's paw might be broken. We need to prep him for an x-ray."

"Do you want me to hold him down?" I suggested.

"No, Louise can do it," Delilah said as she removed what looked like a bright green squirt gun from a cabinet drawer. As the nurse expertly held the dragon still, the doctor aimed the tool at the dragon's injured leg. A triangular-shaped ray of blue light came out from the end as she waved it over Alonzo's body.

"Is that your x-ray machine?" Eddie asked.

"Yes, it's a medical scanner. It takes a complete body scan of the patient, which uploads to my computer. From there, we can make a proper diagnosis."

I'm not one to mistrust a doctor's ability, but as far as I knew, the good doctor was a people doctor, not a veterinarian. "Uh," I said as I struggled to consider my next words before speaking to Delilah, but nothing came to mind that wouldn't be insulting to her.

"Your Majesty," Delilah said, "this little dragon will be in excellent hands. I worked in veterinary medicine for eighty years before I went back to med school to receive my medical degree."

"What made you switch from pets to people?" I asked.

"People don't bite," the doctor said with a wry grin.

After leaving Alonzo in the infirmary, Eddie and I went to our room. I held his hand as we walked. "You have a soft spot for Alonzo," I told him.

"No, I don't," he lied.

"Then what do you call your act of heroism in the roc's nest?"

"I was worried about your emotional state if he had been eaten."

I looked at him. "You know I can read your mind."

"What is my mind saying?"

I knew exactly what he was thinking. Peering into his mind, I saw his thoughts drifted back to his childhood. "Alonzo reminds you of the catnip dragon your mother had when you were a kid, but he is less annoying and cuter than that intolerable Puddles. Wow! Your mom really named him Puddles?"

"Actually, that's what I called him. His real name was Fluffers."

"I like the name Puddles."

"Let's just say that his actions gave him that nickname."

I laughed. "Does this mean you're inclined to keep Alonzo if none of Reckless Randy's friends or family shows up to claim him?"

He smiled, "Yeah, Alonzo seems like a good catnip dragon. He waited for us by the backpack and, even in his own stupid way, tried to take on the roc."

"If we do end up keeping him, I'm pretty sure he's litterbox-trained." I entered our room, went to use the bathroom while Eddie sat on the bed, and began taking out the Tomlinsons from the backpack. It was quiet for a few moments until I was in the middle of washing my hands when I heard Eddie say, "Crap!"

"What's wrong?"

"There are no red and green wires!"

I dried my hands on a towel and walked into our room. My husband had kicked off his shoes and was sitting cross-legged on the bed. He had popped open the bottom of the umbrellas with his penknife and was staring at it with frustration. I sat next to him. "What are you going to do?"

"Fiddle around with the wires until I fix it," he answered as he inserted a small pair of wire cutters into the inside of the handle and snipped two of the wires. He spent the rest of the flight back to Mount Hottah working on the umbrellas while I took a little catnap.

Chapter Eight:
Guessing Riddles Can Be Hazardous to Your Health

Our next quest sent us to a large island on the outer reaches of the queendom. The Monte Carlo dropped Eddie and me off on a dilapidated pier. The second our feet touched the rotten wood, the planks creaked and groaned underneath. Not wanting to fall through another hole, we sprinted across the wood and on to solid ground. I watched in astonishment as the pier disintegrated behind us. "Well, that could've gone horribly wrong," I muttered.

"That would be the second time we nearly fell through rotten wood."

"This does not bode well for the safety rankings on this

particular quest."

Eddie nodded in agreement as he looked around for the location of the next firestone. He finally spotted a large, old building about fifty yards ahead of us. "Borque Gymnasium straight ahead."

"Onward!" I said as I took the first step. To my surprise, my foot sank a few inches into the ground but came back up dry. I took another curious but hesitant step. The same result. "Weird," I said.

"What is it?" Eddie asked.

"Not sure," I replied, squatting down to inspect the strange, pinkish ground. I pressed my hand and found it dry but very bouncy. "I think the entire island is on a bog."

My husband joined me and tested the ground himself. "You're right.

"I know what this is," I said excitedly. "We're about to walk on an island made of spongiam."

"Say what?"

"It's a sponge-like organism that grows from the sea. Over time, the spongiam attaches itself to another organism and takes it over." I led him over to a nearby tree. "See this?"

"Yes, it's a tree."

I shook my head. "Nope. Touch it."

He touched the bark and pulled his hand back in surprise. "It feels like I'm touching a sponge."

I continued with my self-proclaimed PBS special. "Once the metamorphosis is complete, the only thing that is left from the other organism is its physical appearance. Kind of like that doppelganger we had to deal with."

Eddie looked at me in bewilderment. "How do you know this?"

"Someone returned a children's book about it at the library."

"Your ability to spout off obscure knowledge never ceases to amaze me."

"I know. I scare myself sometimes."

As we squished our way to an abandoned, oblong building, I asked Eddie about Borque Gymnasium. "The name sounds really familiar. Hasn't Dirk mentioned him before?" Dirk is my tech-savvy brother-in-law.

"Yeah, according to Dirk, he's an eccentric billionaire who made his first million in developing some computer programs for the blind. Borque decided to start the Borque School for Excellence, a tech college."

I looked around for some more buildings, but I got nothing. "This isn't much of a school."

"Dirk told me Borque gave up after the contractors quit due to some rumors of vicious creatures which had taken up residence in one of the finished buildings."

"With our luck, it'll be this one," I said.

Eddie nodded in agreement.

"So, what happened with Borque?"

"I guess he's made out pretty well for himself with the enormous success of his online college." We had arrived at the entrance of the gym and stood before the giant fiberglass doors. Eddie tugged on the handles, which squished, in his hands. "It looks like the spongiam has overtaken the gymnasium." He gave up on using the doorknob and pushed the doors open with his shoulder.

When we walked inside, the large gym had transformed

into a large, multicolored sponge. The floor moved up and down like a nearly deflated bounce-house as we walked around. The moonlight pierced through little holes in the building's interior, leaving a disco ball effect. We ended up putting on our headlamps to begin our search for the firestone. "Hey, what color is this firestone supposed to be?" My husband asked after a few moments.

"Blue."

"Found it."

I followed the beam from Eddie's headlamp to a clear box embedded in the ceiling. The gemstone's hue bounced off the light and sent blue sparkles everywhere. "That was easy," I said. As a vampire, I could easily leap a good ten-foot span. I decided to give it a chance. I readied myself and jumped a good two feet in the air. "Crap!" I said. "The floor is affecting my jumping. How are we going to get it down?"

"Let me try," Eddie offered. At first, he was going to do the jump himself but had a better plan. "Nebulae," my husband said as he conjured up a baseball-size blue ball of energy. He took a pitcher's stand and threw it at the box. The only thing that was accomplished was creating a sudden tremor throughout the entire gym.

"Uh, honey," I said, "let's not bring the entire building down upon our heads."

"Good thinking, babe." We looked up at the ceiling and considered our next move. "If your dad was here, he could just stretch himself to the ceiling and grab the box."

"Well, he's not here," I said bitterly.

"Did you even invite him and your stepmom to the coronation?"

"No."

"Shelly—," he started to say, but I cut him off.

"Eddie, he lied to me about my mother and my sister."

My husband put his arms around me. "I know, and I know how much that hurt you."

Tears came to my eyes, but I brushed them away quickly. About a month ago, my world was turned upside down when I found out that I was next in line for the throne of a hidden queendom. What had hurt me the most was that my father, my deceased mother, and my stepmother never told me about my long-lost twin sister. Of course, the sisterly reunion had nearly gotten both Eddie, and I killed.

"You have a great relationship with your father. You can't stay mad at him forever," he said, interrupting my thoughts. "I've been there. Being estranged from your parents is tough. It tears you up inside. I just don't want to see you go through that."

I gave a great sigh, knowing he was right. When he was turned into a vampire, his Welkie mother disowned him. "I know, but I can't deal with it right now."

"Okay," Eddie replied, "but when you're ready to talk with him and Amelia, we'll do it together." He pushed his father-in-law's problems to the back of his mind for the time being. "Let's deal with this."

We were silent for a long time, contemplating the release of the firestone. "I think I might be able to reach it if you give me a boost," I finally said.

He thought about it. "That just might work." He squatted down and laced his hands together as I backed up a few steps. "Ready?"

I nodded and broke into a sprint. I leaped into his hands

and flew up in the air as he tossed me up towards the firestone. All vampires can crawl up walls like a spider. I punched a hole through the ceiling as I grabbed a handful of sponge. "Okay, I'm there!" I shouted to Eddie as I inspected the transparent box that held the firestone. The blue lights blinked on four locks similar to the devices you see in the electronics department in retail stores. I tugged at the box. A loud, female computerized voice came from one of the buttons. "Would you like to answer the riddle?"

"What?" I asked.

"That is not a valid response," the voice said. "Would you answer the riddle?"

Eddie glanced up at the devices. "I've seen these before. They're called riddle locks. It's a type of security system. The boxes are held down by magic and can only be deactivated by selecting the right answer to the riddle."

"What happens when you select the wrong answer?" I asked.

"You have two chances to guess correctly," Eddie replied.

"What happens on the third chance?"

"Let's just say I want to leave here in one piece."

I turned to the box. "Yes, I would like to answer the riddle."

"Please answer the following riddle: "I run but cannot walk. I sometimes sing but never talk. I lack arms, have hands, lack a head but have a face. What am I?"

"Oh, that's easy," I said. "A clock."

"Correct answer," the voice said. The first blue light changed to green.

"Would you like to answer the second riddle?" the computerized voice asked.

I was about to answer when a shadowy, winged creature darted past me just out of my line of sight. I swept the room with my flashlight beam. "Hello? Who's there?" A thunderous WAK-WAK, WAK-WAK filled the room as our flashlight beams flew around, searching for the thing making the noise. The noise slowly died away. A report on mythological creatures I did in high school flooded into my mind. "Oh, crap," I said to myself.

Eddie heard my oath. "Shelly, is everything all right?"

"We're not alone. Something is up on the ceiling with me."

"It could be a homeless Winged One."

I shone my flashlight on the ceiling around me. "Nope," I

said, looking straight ahead. I placed my free hand on the hilt of my sword.

"What do you mean?"

"It's not a Winged One."

"What makes you so sure?"

"Three things," I said, still looking at the hideous creature in front of me. "Number one: Winged Ones can't climb up walls like a spider. Number two: They don't have split bluish tongues about a foot long. And number three: I'm pretty sure they can't pull a Linda Blair like this aswang up here."

Eddie's eyes followed my eyes to a dark grey creature with enormous bat-like wings. Long, curved claws dug into the ceiling as it hung there, staring at us with unblinking, completely red eyes. Its tongue darted in and out of a lipless mouth. The bald head spun another 360 degrees as it stealthily and slowly moved closer to me. "We need to get out of here," Eddie said.

"The aswang hasn't separated itself. We're not in danger, yet," I assured the vampire.

"Shell," my husband asked, "what happens when it does?"

"We run like Scooby and Shaggy," I said.

"You seem to know a lot about these creatures, Shelly," Eddie said. He slowly reached for the shortened war scythe on his utility belt. He gave it a quick shake as it extended to its full length.

"I happened to do a paper on them in high school, but my teacher said they were too violent for a report."

"Did your research give any clues about their habits or anything? Such as: Are they solitary creatures? What is their diet?"

"They eat flesh and blood. Very vague on their lifestyles, and I think they are impossible to kill."

"Wow, very reassuring, Shelly," Eddie said dryly.

"Let's keep calm and get this firestone," I said.

My husband looked at me with skepticism. "Is staying calm a way to avoid their attack?"

"Nope, just common sense," I said.

I glanced over my shoulder see the aswang silently stalking me. The same electronic voice spoke up. "Would you like to answer the riddle?"

"You gotta be kidding me! Another freaking riddle?" I

exclaimed. I gave a sigh. "Yes, I would like to answer the riddle."

"Please answer the following riddle: I was carried into a dark room and set on fire. I wept, and then my head was cut off. What am I?"

"A match?" I guessed.

"Incorrect answer."

"One of these creatures," Eddie said.

"Incorrect answer."

Not helping, I mentally told Eddie. I motioned him to be quiet as I concentrated on the puzzle. A match could be set on fire, but the rest of the puzzle didn't fit. What could be set on fire, but weep? Then the answer came to me. "A candle."

"Correct answer."

I was confronted with another riddle. "With pointed fangs, I sit in wait. With piercing force, I dole out fate. Over bloodless victims, proclaiming might. Eternally joining with a single bite. What am I?"

I was utterly stumped. "Any ideas?"

"Ah, Shelly, we have a slight problem."

No kidding, I thought.

"Our scary friend just invited three of his buddies."

"As long as they don't—."

Too late. Half of the aswangs began closing in on us. Literally, the creatures' upper halves started splitting from the rest of them, leaving behind bloody, nasty trails of various internal organs. The lower halves remained motionless, sticking to the ceiling.

Eddie touched a button on his bracelet, and an impenetrable, metal shield popped up. He brought his war scythe down one of the aswang's necks. Nothing happened. It was as if the creature's neck was made of metal.

"These guys can separate their torsos! I'm pretty sure decapitation's not going to work on them!" I shouted. I went back to working on the riddle when I felt a slimy, ropey tongue wrapped around my neck. I was yanked back away from the firestone. Panicking, I felt around for something to cut the powerful tongue. My fingers brushed against something round and metal. The chakrams had better work! I managed to unclip one from my belt and flung the metal ring at the creature with a backward flip of my wrist.

The aswang let out a surprised shriek that nearly blew out my eardrums. The long tongue quickly unwrapped itself from my neck. I scrambled back to the firestone just as the computer voice told me that I had said the wrong answer. I quickly thought about the riddle again when the answer came to me. "A stapler! It's a stupid stapler! Happy now?"

"Correct answer," the voice said.

"Hey, Shell," Eddie called up to me as he slammed the edge of his shield into one of the aswangs' faces, "quick question: why on earth did you pick these things as subjects for your report?"

"Actually, vampires were my first pick, but my teacher said they were too violent."

"We're not violent," Eddie replied as he took another failed attempt at decapitating one of the beasts.

One of the aswangs leaped on my back. Its claws dug into my skin like a thousand needles as it bit into the soft spot of my shoulder. I let out a shout of pain. It let go the moment I elbowed it in the face. "Then I picked aswangs because they were my second choice, but they were too gruesome."

"What did you end up picking?" Eddie asked. One of the beasts slammed into him at full speed and knocked him on the ground. It tried to eat his face, but he managed to kick it off.

"Unicorns, really boring subject," I said. I touched the last lock, and the voice asked if I wanted to answer the final riddle. "No! I enjoy being attacked by flying, flesh-eating creatures," was what I wanted to say, but I said yes instead.

"I am the ruler of shovels. I have a double. I am thin as a knife. I have a wife. What am I?"

Great, the last riddle, and my mind was completely blank like a sheet of paper. I could smell my blood seeping from my shoulder wound, and I was almost positive the aswangs' teeth and claws had some sort of poison in them and were probably sweeping through my bloodstream at this very moment

"The king of spades! That's the answer!" Eddie shouted to me. He was pinned to the ground by one of the creatures. It slashed and clawed at his face and chest. He turned into mist before his face was clawed off and slipped out from under the aswang. When he finally materialized, blood was running down his face and chest from deep cuts.

"King of spades!" I shouted at the computerized voice.

"Correct answer!" The lock blinked off, the box opened up, and the firestone dropped into my waiting hands. "Got it!" I shouted to my husband as I shoved the troublesome jewel into my infinity fanny pack. I let go of the ceiling and dropped to the floor. Unfortunately, I landed unsteadily on my feet as I swore the poison was attacking my immune system. Note to self: Vampires can get seriously ill from aswang venom. I shook myself and joined my husband, who had backed himself up against a wall. He wasn't looking too hot himself.

"What now?" Eddie asked as he took another failed swipe at the creatures.

The old saying, "Music hath charms to soothe the savage beast," popped into my swimming head. I fished out my smartphone and scrolled through the apps, all the while silently praying that I could a signal here. I found what I was looking for and hit play. Soft instrumental music filled the room as the aswangs stopped in mid-flight and cocked their heads in curiosity. They hung in mid-air for a few long moments before gathering their torsos and dreamily flying into the darkness. Then like birds, they tucked their heads under their wings and began to what I took for snoring. "Okay," I whispered, "let's be super quiet and get out of here. I'll keep the music going." We hurried out of the building in one piece.

When we teleported back to the airship, we were immediately rushed to the infirmary. About forty minutes later, Eddie and I were healing with the help of blood for me and juice for him, along with a unicorn salve applied to our wounds. The infirmary had given us extra scrub tops as our shirts were in tatters. We rested as the airship took us back to Hiram's.

Tired and in minimal pain, my husband and I stood in Laban's presence as he paraded around his own personal throne room. The pamola was dressed in a Louis XVIII get-up. "Here's your firestone," I said, resisting the urge to chuck it at his head.

The pamola stopped sauntering around the room. He grabbed the gem from me and tossed it carelessly onto the floor along with the two others. "Now, the coordinates for the next firestone are—."

I looked around for Hiram, but the other pamola was nowhere in sight. "Wait a minute!" I interrupted as I held up a hand. "Where is Hiram?"

He shrugged apathetically. "Don't know, don't care. I have the coordinates for the next firestone."

"No, I will only speak to Hiram," I said.

"He's unavailable."

The anger inside me was threatening to explode, but somehow I managed to keep my cool. "I'm going home. I'll be back here by ten tomorrow morning. If you want me to retrieve the rest of the firestones for you, Hiram will be the only one giving me the coordinates. Do we have an understanding?"

"Yes, yes. Now go back to your little hovel." He waved us away like annoying gnats.

When my husband and I got to our castle, we were exhausted and very irritated when we saw Doctor Orlok sitting on a green and blue plaid loveseat just inside the main doors. He got up and blocked out our way to our private elevator. "Your

Majesty, I demand to speak with you about your ill-fated plan to retrieve the firestones."

I looked at my watch and then back at Doctor Orlock. I already had to deal with one sanctimonious idiot and wasn't in the mood to deal with another. "Do you have any idea what time it is?"

"Your Majesty, this is very important."

"It's almost midnight. I am sore and exhausted. Can this wait until tomorrow?"

"No, it cannot. I want to know why you didn't explain your plan in full detail to the cabinet."

"And I want peace on earth and a less annoying Minister of Virtue, and I know I'm not getting either one anytime soon," I was tempted to say if I wasn't a queen. My sense of royal duties prevailed over my sense of sarcasm. "I told the cabinet I had a plan to get to the firestones."

"But you refused to tell me what the plan is."

I repressed an irritated growl. "As I told you and the other cabinet members, I don't want to divulge my plan because I'm not sure if it will work."

"Your sister would've told me everything. I was one of her confidants. She was a much better queen than you are turning out to be."

"My sister is a raving psychopath who would execute and destroy anyone who stands in her way. So, Doctor Orlock, I am much better a queen than she ever was! Once I get the firestones and rescue the prime minister, I'll tell the cabinet everything. Do I make myself clear?"

"No, I insist that—."

I looked at my husband. "Eddie, what do you think Ra and Apophis' moods will be if we wake them?"

"Not good," Eddie replied. "I've heard if you wake sphinxes up, they can be very, very, very cranky."

"Almost homicidal," I remarked. I stole a glance at the minister of virtue.

"Fine!" Dr. Orlock snapped. "I'll go, but this conversation isn't over." He stormed out of the castle's main doors without giving us a second look.

"Of course, it isn't. I haven't got all the firestones yet," I muttered just loud enough for Eddie to hear.

The large, heavy wooden doors slammed shut, and the noise reverberated throughout the castle. My husband looked at me. "Wow! I can't believe him."

"His audacity is astounding," I said as I rubbed my tired eyes.

"I think he's going to be a big problem in the near future," Eddie said as we walked to the elevator that led to our private quarters. He hit the up button with his thumb. "I'm reminded of that quote from the Godfather."

I nodded and leaned against the love of my life as he wrapped his arms around me. We got on the elevator and rode it up to our suite. "'Leave the gun, take the cannoli?'"

"No, but that's a good line," he said with a smile. "The line I was thinking of is 'keep you friends close, but your enemies closer.' Now, I want a cannoli."

"Me too," I replied as we walked into our bedroom. Our unmade mattress was still on the floor. "Okay, I'm going to ask a couple members of the staff to put together our bed. Sleeping on the floor reminds me of camping."

"I know how much you love camping."

"Yeah, the lure of sleeping under the stars, listening to the peaceful sounds of the animals roaming the forest at night, waking up with a sore back in the morning because you slept on a root the night before fills me with endless joy. And let's not forget the best part of camping: Getting up in the middle of the night to use the bathroom and the closest restroom is an outhouse twenty miles away from your campsite."

"Okay," my husband said as he took an imaginary pen and a pad of paper and pretended to write. "Note to self: Never, ever take you camping."

I gave him a passionate kiss and whispered in his ear as I ran my fingers through his curly hair. "I don't mind camping out right here on our bed."

Eddie grinned as we fell onto the mattress. "Au naturel?" he asked.

Chapter Nine:
Near-Death By a Thousand Slinkys

Hiram sits at a long table covered with all kinds of food.

Ham, roasted duck, lemon curry chicken, Thanksgiving turkeys

in platters of all shapes and sizes. Mounds of fruit are piled up in

fancy large bowls. Honey-glazed carrots, spinach au gratin,

roasted garlic squash, toasted orzo, and enough other vegetable

dishes were there to satisfy any vegetarian's tastes. Cupcakes,

strawberry shortcakes, pies, and other delectable pastries on

plates and bowls are scattered about the table. In the middle of

the table is a large bouquet of flowering weeds.

The pamola reaches for a piece of chicken. As he is about

to put it in his mouth, it vanishes before him. He takes a banana,

but before he can take a bite, it rots immediately. Each piece of food Hiram either tries to eat rots or vanishes before he can take a bite. Soon the entire table is empty of food. "Laban," Hiram pleads, "please let me have something to eat."

Laban sits at the other end, devouring all the food. He laughs, spitting out crumbs as he speaks. "Hiram, Hiram, you're not hungry. You're thirsty. Have a cold glass of water."

Hiram does as suggested. When he brings the silver goblet filled with cool, refreshing water to his lips, the liquid turns to sand. He spills it out onto the tablecloth and refills his glass. Again, the liquid is turned to sand. He repeats the process until all of the pitchers of water are emptied.

Hiram reaches for the bouquet, but Laban causes it to disappear. "No!" Hiram screams, "I need that to heal!" Then Laban makes the entire table vanish, and Hiram is transported to a dingy cell.

I woke from the vision two hours before our alarm went off. I glanced over at my husband, who was still sleeping. I tried to get back to sleep, but nothing prevailed. There was no need to wake Eddie. I gave him a kiss on the cheek, grabbed a purple and white striped T-shirt, jeans and underwear before heading into the shower.

I had an epiphany while I was in the shower. Laban was most definitely starving Hiram. The prime minister was very much emaciated when we first saw him in his cage. The bouquet of weeds was significant. Ever since I found out I could have visions, I've learned to pay attention to the smallest details in them. Perhaps the weeds had some healing powers. I would have to research my theory further.

First things first, Hiram would need some food. I slipped quietly down to the main kitchen. The smell of cooked fish drifted through the air, and I suddenly craved baked fish. Standing on a stepstool, a white-haired dwarf in a chef's uniform was chopping up apples on a glass cutting board on a large, marble island with six bar stools. "Good morning, your Majesty," she said without looking up from her task.

"Good morning—." I paused as I tried to remember her name. Mary? Maria? Mabel! That was it! "Mabel. What are you making?"

"Fapple pie." She pointed to a pie sitting on the counter

behind her.

"Don't you mean apple pie?" I asked, thinking I misheard her.

"Nope, fapple pie. An old royal recipe. Every queen loved this recipe, including your sister."

"Would you like a slice?" She cut me a piece of pie and placed it on a crystal plate.

"Maybe for dessert," I said. "I actually need some food for an ill friend."

"What kind of food?"

"Your basic food with vitamins, minerals, and nutrition."

"Check the refrigerator and the pantry," the chef replied. "What would you and the king like for breakfast?"

"Oatmeal would be fine."

"I have cinnamon maple brown oatmeal with raisins."

"Sounds great." After rummaging for a paper bag, I went to the refrigerator and gathered some bananas, apples, a loaf of bread, some cheese, and bottled water. For some reason, I grabbed two cans of Vienna sausages from the pantry.

"Mabel, why is an entire cupboard dedicated to cocktail

wieners?" I asked.

"Oh, Queen Rachel won a lifetime supply of them last year."

"Why?"

The dwarf shrugged. "I don't know, your Majesty."

Okay, mildly disturbing, I thought to myself.

"What would you and your husband like for supper tonight?"

"Oh, don't worry about us," I said as I sat down on a barstool next to the kitchen island. "We can feed ourselves. Is there a nearby grocery store?"

"Your Majesty, you are going to be busy for the next few days. Let the staff prepare your meals this week."

"All right, fine with me. I'll talk with Eddie tonight, and we'll make a menu." One of my many brilliant ideas came to me. Mabel might know about the healing powers of weeds. "Mabel," I asked the chef, "how long have you worked for the royal family?"

"Sixty years. Like many of your staff, my family has been employed here for generations."

"So you must know some pretty good stories."

She nodded.

"I've heard the story of how the first queen met Hiram, but I'm curious of how she nursed the prime minister back to help."

"According to the story, she gave him medicine made of flowering weeds."

"Really? How was the medicine made?"

She thought about it for a few moments. "I don't know, but I'm sure it's recorded somewhere in the royal archives."

"Where would those be?"

"The royal library upstairs."

I gathered up the food. "Thank you. I'll take a look there just to satisfy my curiosity. We'll be down for breakfast in thirty minutes."

The cook nodded and went back to making her pie.

I walked up a flight of stairs and took the long hallway to the library. When I opened the door, I was greeted by empty, warping shelves. I sighed as I remembered my sister had flooded or burned almost everything in this room. I began to wonder if she had the gall to destroy the royal archives. "Maybe there's a secret room here," I said to myself. I walked along the wall, tapping every foot for a hollow sound.

"What are you doing?"

I stopped and turned around to see my husband standing in the doorway. He was showered and dressed in a green T-shirt, blue Leviathan jeans, and sneakers. I walked over to him and gave him a long kiss as I wrapped my arms around his neck. "Good morning, love."

"Good morning, babe. The chef told me you were in here," he said after we broke our kiss. "What's going on?"

"I'm looking for a secret room that holds the royal archives," I told him about the dream and my theory.

"You're right," Eddie replied as he joined me in the search. "Hiram's definitely not staying at the Ritz Carlton."

"I think the weed bouquet might be a medicine for him. I just need to find out how to make it. I just hope my ancestor wrote it down in the royal scrolls somewhere." I stopped along the wall just as I heard a hollow sound. "I think I found it." Looking down, I spotted a golden door stopper against the wall with no door in sight. I nudged the doorstop with the toe of my sneaker, and it let out a satisfying BOING. A section of the library's wall slid open to reveal a hidden room about the size of a darkened broom closet.

Eddie turned on the flashlight app on his smartphone, "Well, that sucks," he announced.

"Yep," I agreed as we stared at cartons upon cartons, which were marked only with a combination of numbers and letters. "How many boxes do you think are in here?"

"A lot. Probably the entire room is full of them."

"Great, and I thought this was going to be easy. Going through these is going to be a pain in the rear."

"Shelly, before we spend hours, even days, sifting through this stuff, we should ask for help."

"That is an excellent idea, Eddie," I said a little too enthusiastically. "Woo-hoo! Less work for me."

"Most likely more work for a certain private secretary."

"I was just going to ask him about it. He might know the exact box we're looking for."

Fortunately, Gunther did know. During the Demon Wars,

he and his father had packed up all the royal archives and hid them in the library. The satyr had told us this while we were on our way back to Mount Hottah. "It might take me about an hour to locate the box," he said over the phone. He had insisted on staying behind at Castle DeLorean. "You know how to operate the item I gave you?"

"Piece of cake," Eddie replied.

"Good luck to the both of you, your Majesties."

When Eddie and I arrived at Hiram's home, Laban had made himself an ivory and gold throne and was sitting on it, still wearing his ridiculous King Louis XVI outfit. "I talked to Hiram this morning, and he gave me the coordinates to the next firestone," he gleefully told us.

"I'm sure he did, but I would like to get them from him," I said to Laban. "Where is Hiram?"

Laban lazily snapped his fingers, and the stasis field appeared. His brother lay on the floor. His black and white striped prison uniform hung loosely from his shoulders.

"We want to speak with Hiram alone," I told Laban.

"Release him and leave us."

"Fine," Laban said as he made the cage disappear.

Eddie stood guard and watched him leave through the mouth of the cave. "We're clear," he told me as he took off his backpack. He handed me a banana and a bottle of water.

I helped Hiram to a sitting position and gave him some water, which he drank greedily. "Take it slow, Mr. Prime Minister," I told him. I handed him the banana and waited as he scarfed it down. "What are the coordinates for the next firestone?"

He wiped the excess water from his mouth with the back of his hand before giving the latitudes and longitudes. He looked at me suspiciously. "What are you doing giving the firestones to my brother?"

"I've got a plan. Just trust me,"

"Why should I trust a member of the royal family?" he demanded.

"Because I'm the only one who is going to rescue you."

Hiram gave a reluctant sigh. "I guess I have no choice."

"The flowering weeds," I said quietly. "How do they heal you?"

The prime minister was about to speak when a bolt of lightning struck him in the side. I could smell the electricity as it whizzed inches away from my head

Laban stormed into the cave and released some more lightning, electrocuting his brother. "How dare you give Hiram some food? I am taking care of him!"

I scrambled to my feet. I saw Eddie draw his war scythe, but I held out my hand and mentally told him to stay where he was but be on his guard. I stood in front of Hiram and drew my sword. I aimed its sharp tip at Laban. "Hiram is under my protection." I kept my voice steady and robust, which betrayed the anger threatening to emerge. "You will give me your word that you no longer hurt him."

"I don't take orders from a terrestrial," snarled Laban.

Eddie got fed up with just standing there. He drew his war scythe and quickly placed himself between Laban and me. His voice was dangerously calm. "Actually, she is your queen, and I strongly advise you to listen to her."

"What if I don't?"

I forced myself not to wince at Laban's stupid retort.

Eddie's never in a good mood when someone tries to kill me. "Let's just say you don't want to find out," the vampire said. Then he gave Laban a dangerous, fanged smile before we left the cave.

An hour and a half later, Eddie and I found ourselves standing on the edge of a bizarrely looking cliff. It wasn't even a mountain, just a very tall stone structure the width of a school. I peered down the dizzying drop-off. "We must be at least a thousand miles high," I said, masking my fear

Winds whipped wildly around us as my husband double-checked the figure-eight knot on the anchor attached to the top rope. "Probably more like a mile," he replied. He noticed my nervousness. "You okay?"

"I've never done this before, Eddie."

He placed a fingerless gloved hand on my shoulder. "You'll be fine. I'm right here every step of the way."

I swallowed hard as I ran my fingers up and down the green and yellow nylon webbing attached to my harness and ropes via the carabiners. "What if we fall?"

"The belay devices will catch and stop the fall. Also, we have these guys to grab the rope." He jerked his thumb to the two crewmembers of the Monte Carlo.

The gorillas were brothers, Ron and Mel McDowall. "Don't worry about a thing, your Majesty. If anything happens, Ron and I will pull you up. Just give us the word."

By using a powerful searchlight aboard the airship, we had spotted the firestone embedded in the side of the cliff. Eddie and the chief engineer had come up with a complex mathematical system to pinpoint the firestone's exact location, while I had just nodded and smiled when appropriate. "Shelly, remember what I told you about rappelling?" Eddie asked as he prepared to step backward off the edge of the cliff.

"Walk down. How far is it to the firestone?"

"About three hundred feet. We have at least four hundred feet of rope in case our calculations are off." I must have turned a few shades of white because my husband gave me a concerned look. "Are you sure you're up to this? Because I can get the firestone by myself."

"I'm fine," I lied.

Eddie gave my hand a reassuring squeeze. "I'll be with you every step of the way." He stepped back to the edge of the cliff. "Ready?"

I nodded. Together we stepped off the cliff and began rappelling down the edge. I didn't realize how tightly I was clinging to the rope until Eddie told me to ease up. I stupidly glanced down for a moment and nearly threw up with fright. I had fought zombies, dinosaurs, and other scary creatures, but looking down a thousand-foot drop-off still scared the pants off me. Even vampires would never survive a fall like that. Looking up made me feel more ill, and I decided to look straight ahead at the rock face. There were perfectly round holes embedded into the stone. I wanted to get a closer look at them, but we were going too fast.

Once we saw the tip of the firestone jutting out from the rock, Eddie spoke into his earpiece, letting the gorillas know to stop giving us more rope. "Hey, Shelly, you ready to pry this bad boy from this rock?" he shouted to me over the roar of the winds.

I shook my head vigorously as I found myself clinging to the rope with a death grip. "Why don't you do it?"

Eddie nodded, taking in my terrified state. He unclipped the small steel hammer pick from my belt and began to tap away at the rock surrounding the firestone. "Placing your hand and feet on the rock face might ease your fears, babe," he said.

I lifted up my head the moment I heard a strange sound. It sounded like a piece of metal being snapped back and forth in the wind. Remembering a vampire's ability to cling to walls like a spider, I let go of my rope and clung to the rock face. To take my mind off a possible long fall to my death, I decided to investigate the rock face. I peered inside the closest hole and spotted a rainbow-colored coiled spring sitting in the back. "Someone left a Slinky in here. A little dusty, but I bet it works fine."

Eddie had finished hammering and was now prying the firestone loose. "A Slinky?"

"Yeah, the compressed spring toy," I began to sing, much to my husband's annoyance. "What walks downstairs, alone or in pairs and makes a slinkity sound? A spring, a spring, a marvelous thing! Everyone knows it's Slinky. It's Slinky, it's Slinky, It's fun, it's a wonderful toy. It's Slinky, it's Slinky, it's fun, It's a wonderful toy. It's fun for a girl or a boy."

"Thanks for that lovely song, babe," Eddie replied dryly as he unzipped my infinity fanny pack and placed the gemstone inside.

"Didn't your parents ever buy you a Slinky when you were a kid?"

"By the time Slinkys came out, I was in college."

"Oh, that's right. I keep forgetting how old you are." I smiled at him. "That's it. I'm getting you two Slinkys for your birthday."

"Two?"

"Yes, so we can have Slinky races down the castle's stairs."

Eddie peeked into the hole nearest him. "You don't have to wait for my birthday. I found another Slinky."

I was transfixed in stunned horror as the Slinky began to move of its own free will. Four red wiggly eyes fastened their gaze on me before it flipped forward. Tiny, razor-sharp teeth retracted inside and outside the coils as it began rapidly moving towards me. "Forget about the Slinky!"

He reached inside for it and quickly pulled his hand back.

"Don't touch it!"

I looked at Eddie. The creature had latched onto his arm like one of those bangle bracelets. Small trails of blood dripped from his arm.

"Watch out!" I shouted as I removed one of my chakrams and flung it at the creature on my husband's arm. The weapon sliced cleanly through the Slinky's body as Eddie turned himself into a mist. When he rematerialized, the now-deceased creature tumbled down the drop-off. "I think we're good," I said to Eddie.

He looked up. "I don't think so, Shell."

I followed his gaze as hundreds of Slinky creatures came out of the holes and descended upon us. We tried to pull them off, but they wrapped their springy bodies around our necks as they entangled themselves. The more we yanked them off, the more kept coming. A long, agonizing few minutes passed before we were able to get rid of most of them.

I heard the terrifying sound of the rope snapping and looked up to see one of the things had wrapped its body around Eddie's belay line. The teeth had nearly cut through the rope fibers. I managed to grab my husband's hand before the rope broke free. My heart nearly dropped when he almost slipped out of my grasp, but he quickly clung to the wall as he wrapped his free arm around my waist.

"Eddie," I said, "I don't have a plan to get out of here."

"Fortunately, I do. Cut your rope."

"What?"

"Trust me and hang on to me."

I took a deep breath and sliced the remaining rope with my chakram.

Eddie pushed off hard from the rock face, and we began plummeting downwards. "Citadel!" he shouted. A green force field immediately enclosed around us.

I looked at my husband in horror. Could his force field survive the impact once we hit the ground? More importantly, could we survive the impact? I really hoped he had some flying spells leftover from his wizarding days.

Instead, he reached for one of the Tomlinsons he had clipped on to his belt and dissipated the force field before uttering the magic words to teleport us back to the Monte Carlo.

When we arrived on the airship, Cassius was in the middle of chewing out Ron and Mel. The captain stopped mid-lecture to stare at us with a mixture of relief and horror. "Kill those things!" he ordered.

"Hey!" Eddie started to protest when he noticed the two creatures wrapped around my entire right leg.

I looked down at the blood running down my pant leg. "Can someone get these off me, please?"

Cassius pulled a dagger from his belt and expertly cut off the living Slinkys. He saw me staring at the bloodless, lifeless coils on the floor. "They're called Mufflewumps, your Majesty. Nasty little vermin. They live on cliffs in round holes."

"We must have disturbed a nest of them when we got the firestone," I said weakly.

Cassius nodded. "You and the king need to get down to the infirmary to get those wounds taken care of."

We obeyed the captain's orders and limped our way to the infirmary. Eddie looked at me. "Shelly, I've decided I don't want Slinkys for my birthday."

"I don't blame you one bit, Eddie."

Chapter Ten:
Revenge of the Plants

With the way our quests had been going, I had the good sense to pack extra clothes. Once our wounds were bandaged and had begun to heal, we went back to our room and changed into clean clothes. I considered charging Hiram for replacement clothes. We delivered the firestone and were given the coordinates for the next quest, which turned out to be right on the main island.

Cassius dropped us off at the hangar so he and the crew could fuel up and get some much-needed rest. Eddie and I drove to the coast of the island. We bumped along an unkempt dirt driveway littered with potholes. My husband put the car in park and shut off the engine as we looked at the massive structure in front of us. The 200-feet high building looked like a giant glass golf ball the width and length of two football fields.

"It's a biodome," Eddie said in amazement. "I haven't seen one of these in years."

"A biodome?"

"It's a closed ecological system. Usually, these things have three types of temperatures: tropical, tundra, and coastal. I spent one summer helping a neighbor build one when I was a teenager."

"That was nice of you."

"I was supposed to get paid for all my hard work."

"The neighbor stiffed you?"

"Yep. I was going to use my earnings towards the entry fee for my first car race."

"Did you ever enter the car race?"

"Dirk let me borrow the money from him on the basis that I clean his dragon's stall for a month."

"Couldn't have been that bad. You could've said a spell, and the job would've been done just like that," I said with a snap of my fingers.

"That would've been helpful if I hadn't stupidly agreed to his no-magic rule. Do you know how heavy dragon droppings are?"

I burst out laughing as I pictured my husband being a dragon's personal pooper-scooper. I only managed to get control of myself when my cell phone rang. "Hello!" I said between fits of giggling.

"Your Majesty?" Gunther asked hesitantly.

"Sorry, Gunther," I apologized. "Eddie just told me something funny."

"Okay. I think I might have found the ingredients."

"Excellent, Gunther! I'm putting you on speakerphone." I hit the button. "Can you hear us?"

"Yes, I can. It took me a while, but I found your ancestor's journal. She was able to heal Hiram with a paste made of various weeds. Let me read it to you. 'Hiram's wounds are mortal. I only hope the panax will heal him.' I believe that's the name of the medicine you're looking for. Now, that is the only reference to it for quite some time."

"How long?"

"Fortunately, Queen Aquila wrote down the formula a few years later. Apparently, Hiram was attacked by a creature and nearly died. Your ancestor gave him panax, saving his life once again."

"What was the creature?" I asked.

"It doesn't say, your Majesty. I'll look into it later."

"Don't bother, Gunther. I was just curious."

"Here are the ingredients to the medicine: seven dandelions, two Queen Anne's lace, three thistles, two—."

"Hold it!" I interrupted as I begin to search for a pen and paper in my purse. "I need something to write with."

"No need to," Gunther replied. "I've already sent you and the king the ingredients in an email."

Eddie checked his phone. "Yep, I got it.

"I'm telling you the list to let you know what to expect," the satyr said. He continued with the list. "You'll need two ragweed, six goldenrods, one nightshade, four buttercups, one creeping Charlie, and eight clovers. I've spoken with Dr. Wandasen, and he thinks he might be able to recreate the formula, as long as the materials can be retrieved.”

“That shouldn’t be a problem,” I said. “Eddie and I are outside a bio-dome.”

“What are you doing at the Hermes Conservatory?”

“It’s where the next firestone is.”

“Good luck finding it. The conservatory hasn’t been used for several decades.”

I looked out the windshield at the sparkling bio-dome with the manicured grounds. “It looks like someone’s been taking care of it.”

“Really? Interesting. Dr. Wandasen thinks the best thing to do is to make sure the plants are in pristine condition.”

“But we don’t have anything to put the weeds in,” I said.

“Hold it!” Eddie said as he began to look around the car for a container. He reached into the plastic bag that I insisted he uses as a trash bag and pulled out an empty can of canned potato chips. “I found something that might work.

“Don’t worry, Gunther. We’ll see you in a while.”

“Good luck, your Majesties,” Gunther said before hanging up.

"Thank you, Gunther," I said and signed off. I looked at Eddie. "Let's go get a firestone and some weeds."

"Good thing you added a plural to that word." Eddie and I got out of the car and went around to the back. He popped open the trunk and unzipped a large black duffle bag.

I peered in. "Since when did you add machetes to our weapon collection?"

"A few months ago," he replied as he handed me one.

I mounted it on my belt next to Knowledge. "Glad you brought them. I didn't want to dull my sword on some vines."

Eddie nodded as he strapped on his machete. He glanced over at the biodome with concern. "I wonder who's been taking care of it."

Out of the corner of my eye, I saw something small and green move rapidly through the blossoms of a flowering crabapple tree. "We'll just ask whoever's living in that tree," I suggested. I walked a few feet over to the tree and ducked under the branches. Several tiny doors ran up the length of the trunk. . I crouched down and gave the bottom door a little knock. "Hello?"

My husband grabbed his backpack from the car's trunk

and slung it over his shoulder. He closed the trunk and followed me to the tree. "Shell, what's—Ow!" A crabapple hit him in the cheek.

I looked up in time to have a crabapple nail me right between the eyes. "Ow!" I said.

A high-pitched child's snicker echoed in the branches above Eddie and me. A tiny figure no more than four-inches tall dressed in a green shirt and green pants raced along a nearby branch. A small bag of crabapples was slung over his shoulder.

I got up off the ground and snatched him up in my cupped hands. "Gotcha!" I said. I made a tiny hole with my fingers big enough so he could breathe but not large enough to escape and peered at him.

He looked no more than nine or ten-years-old. "Let me go!" he shouted in a high-pitched voice.

"No," I said, "I caught you fair and square. Don't I get free wishes of some kind?"

He nodded vigorously. "Oh, yes! You get three wishes."

"And a pot of gold," Eddie added. "Don't forget that."

"Yeah, yeah! What's your first wish?"

I knew leprechauns couldn't grant wishes, but this little brat didn't need to know that. "I wish for you to stop throwing crabapples at my husband and me."

"Wait—What? You want to waste your first wish on that?" the kid asked me.

"Yes. First, it hurts when you chuck crab apples at people. Second, it's also rude."

He crossed his arms and huffed. "Fine. Your wish is granted."

Wow, this kid was certainly pouty. "Can I speak to an adult or someone considerably older than you?"

"Why?"

"Can you tell us about the biodome?"

"No!"

"Jasper, quit being a little twerp!" said another young voice. Eddie and I looked up to see a teenaged leprechaun wearing a red t-shirt and jeans sitting on a branch above us. He popped a tiny, red berry in his mouth as he leaned against the tree trunk. "You can squish my little brother," he told me.

"I won't squish him," I said with a smile. I set Jasper down, and he raced to the little door, opened it, and disappeared inside.

I looked up at the older leprechaun. "What's your name?"

He got up, took off his little green fedora, and gave a respectful bow. "Jason Shortstalk, at your service," he said. "And you must be the new queen and king."

I nodded. "Yes, Queen Shelly and King Eddie at your service. We need your help."

Jason grinned. "What can I do?"

"Well, we need to get into the bio-dome."

The teenager was about to say something when an older leprechaun opened one of the doors. He was dressed as a stereotypical leprechaun. "Don't go in there! It's really dangerous!"

"How dangerous?" Eddie asked.

He swallowed. "It's out of control. I warned them."

"Dad," Jason said, "they can rescue him and stop them."

I made a T with my hands in frustration. "Time out. Can you use proper nouns and explain what's going on, please."

"Hendrik Shortstalk, your Majesty," Jason's father introduced himself. "Let me tell you a story." The leprechaun took a little black pipe and a tiny satchel out of his green suit pocket. He took some tobacco out of the bag and stuffed it into his pipe. He reached back into his suit coat and pulled out a book of matches. He broke one off and struck it against the bottom of his shoe. He lit the pipe and tossed the burnt-out match off to the side.

He puffed a few silent minutes before speaking again. "During the Demon Wars, this biodome was ravaged. Most of the roof was destroyed by hellfire and brimstone. One night, amid the Battle for Peregrin, a glowing meteor crashed through the biodome. It opened up, and out spilled strange glowing seeds. These seeds were possessed by an evil-being from beyond."

My husband and I shared a skeptical look. *Evil plants from outer space? Now, I've heard everything*, I told him subliminally.

Hendrik either missed our skeptical glances or chose to ignore them and continued with his tale. "Our friend and protector, Harvey, was curious and went to investigate. When he didn't come back, my eldest sons and I went to look for him. The bio-dome had become infected! The plants were attacking us. Some of them started hunting us. It was as if we were—."

"Wait," I said, "did you say the plants were hunting you?" My jaw just dropped in surprise.

"They had become sentient and were communicating with each other."

"Well, plants do communicate by—."

Hendrik interrupted me. "Have you ever heard of plants talking to each other with grunts and hisses?"

"No," I said. That might be a problem. "Okay, what do you recommend?"

"Don't go in there."

"Well," Eddie said, "that's not an option."

Hendrik eyed my husband warily. "What do you mean?"

"We're on a quest," I said, but I didn't want to go into detail. "We need to collect something of importance."

"Oh! One of the firestones!"

"How did you know about the firestones?"

"We saw Hiram hide a blue one in the bio-dome."

Whom they really saw was Laban, but I kept my mouth shut about that little factoid. "Why didn't you tell anyone?" Because it would've made these quests so much simpler.

"We were terrified. A pamola's powers are beyond anything on this planet."

"As is a pamola's ego," I muttered. "Well, thank you for the information, Hendrik. We'll keep an eye out for Harvey while we're in the bio-dome."

"Dad," Jason asked, "can I go with them?"

Hendrik nearly inhaled his pipe when his son suggested this. After several moments of severe hacking, the patriarch of the Shortstalks looked at his son with dismay. "You know how dangerous it is."

"But the queen and king will protect me," Jason said, "It's her Majesty's royal duty." He looked at me for confirmation. My non-committal shrug didn't help his case as Hendrik slowly shook his head. "I can help find the firestone and Harvey."

"Hold up!" I said as I looked at the teenaged leprechaun. "You can find the firestone? How?"

"We leprechauns can smell valuable metals and minerals," Hendrik said with a grunt.

"We should've come here first, Shelly," Eddie said. "Imagine how much time and effort we could've saved."

"And clothing," I added. "Don't forget that." I looked at Hendrik. "Don't worry. Jason's in good hands."

Hendrik gave a reluctant sigh. "All right, Jason. You can go. Just be careful."

Jason grinned. "Can I ride on your shoulder?" he asked me. When I nodded, he leaped into my open palm.

"Okay, here are the rules," I said as I set the leprechaun on my shoulder. "If this place is as dangerous as you guys say it is, there's a strong possibility that it could get dicey."

"Oh, I'm ready for that," Jason said overconfidently.

"Yeah, I'm not risking your life if you do something stupid. When I say, 'Get in the backpack,' I want you to do it. No questions asked."

The leprechaun gave me a salute. "Yes, ma'am!"

I smiled at him. "All right, let's go!"

We walked to the doors of the bio-dome and tried to open them. They held fast. Eddie tried to peer through the coating of green smudge smeared across the steel doors' fiberglass window. He shouldered the door open only an inch.

A blast of hot, humid air hit us. "Wow! It's like a sauna in there!" I said.

Eddie removed his machete from his belt and began to slice at the greenery. It was an awkward task for him because he could only fit his arm through the door. It took him at least fifteen minutes to cut a large enough area for the door to open several more inches. We squeezed inside but were confronted by a barricade of vines and thorns. "This reminds me of a fairy tale where Prince Charming has to fight his way through enchanted thorns," Eddie said as he continued to slice with his machete.

I felt Jason grip my shirt as I drew my own machete and began to help Eddie with our thorny problems. The humidity in the air must have been one thousand percent. "Didn't the thorns keep growing back?" I asked as I wiped dripping sweat from my eyes.

Eddie managed a shrug. "I was kind of hoping you'd know the answer with your ability to spout off obscure knowledge." His black curls were plastered to his head. "When we back to the castle, I'm taking a shower."

"Me too. My clothes are drenched in sweat." We continued to slice through the vines, which weren't enchanted.

Every time I cut through the plants, I heard a barely perceptible scream. "Do you hear that?" I asked.

My husband stopped mid-swing. "Hear what?" he asked.

"I think the thorns are screaming."

Eddie cut through another branch and listened. Once he heard it, too, his face filled with concern. "Hey, Jason, you might want to get into the backpack." He held out his free hand for the leprechaun to jump onto.

"What's going on?" Jason asked as he leaped onto the vampire's open palm. He unzipped the front pocket of the backpack and slipped inside.

Even though Jason couldn't read Eddie's mind, I could, and we're in so much trouble. "What do you think they're warning us about?" I asked.

"Don't know, but we need to be on our guard." We cut through the thorny barricade in a few minutes and walked into an open area with plants all around us. I was about to speak when Eddie put out a hand to silence me.

What's going on? I asked mentally.

Eddie put away his machete as he cased our

surroundings. *Not sure. You notice how unusually quiet it is in here?* He took the baton off his belt and gave it a quick shake. Immediately his war scythe appeared.

I listened for a little while. There was not even an insect buzzing about the entire bio-dome. *You're right. I don't hear a thing. Very unsettling.* I put my machete away so I could draw Knowledge from its scabbard at a moment's notice. Let's find the firestone, the weeds, and Harvey and get out of here. "Jason, you can get out, but stay on Eddie's shoulder."

The leprechaun scrambled out of the backpack and onto my husband's shoulder. He noticed the war scythe in Eddie's hand. "What's going on, your Majesty?" he asked me.

I didn't answer Jason because I was noticing the plants around us for the first time. Green topiaries in shapes of different animals surrounded the outer edges. A cat, the size of a house, had been designed in a crouching position. A green rhinoceros poised grazing peacefully. There was even a spinosaurus in mid-roar. "Wow! These topiaries are in excellent condition," I said.

"You're right," Eddie said. He glanced over at Jason.

"Who's been taking care of the biodome?"

"No one," replied Jason.

"Disturbing," I said as I bent down to inspect a patch of plants with green lobed leaves and violet funnel-shaped flowers. I wondered if these were any of the weeds needed for Hiram's medicine. "Jason, can you tell me what kind of plants these are?"

"That's Creeping Charlie, just a weed," the leprechaun replied.

"Good. Eddie, do you have a jackknife on you?"

"No, but a throwing star will work just as well." Eddie pulled out one of his silver throwing stars from his utility belt and squatted down next to me. He cut the weed at the base while I unzipped the backpack and took out the chip can.

"I don't think it'll fit in here," I said as I compared the small opening and the large leaves.

Eddie drew a circle in the air with his free hand as he said, "Maximize three." Once the magic spell left his lips, the can grew to three times its size.

"Does the hand waving actually do anything?" Jason

asked.

"It does. It gives the spell pizazz," Eddie said.

I grinned at my husband as I placed the weed into the can. Eddie and I got to our feet and continued searching for more weeds. We only walked a few feet further when I caught some movement out of the corner of my eye. I whirled around and stared at the topiary statues. The cat's tail was now curled in the opposite direction, and the rhino's head was lifted up.

"Is everything okay?" Eddie asked.

"I think the statues are alive."

He looked at them and then at me. "I don't see any difference."

I shook my head. "You're right. I think I might be on edge a little bit."

"Well, various things have tried to kill us in the past couple of days."

I rubbed my eyes. "Just once, can one of these quests be simple and non-lethal?"

"That would be fantastic."

"But with our track record, it will never happen." I bent

down and inspected another clump of plants at our feet. It was a patch of red clovers. I checked my phone for the list. "Okay, we need eight of these."

The next hour, we wandered throughout the bio-dome, gathering the weeds for the Panax formula. Jason would identify the plants, Eddie would cut them, and I would place them in the ever-growing can. It was still tranquil for a garden, not even a bug buzzing or a butterfly fluttering around. What was even more disturbing were the remains of variously sized animals strewed all over the place. The added humidity had increased the smell of decomposition, and it made me wish vampires didn't have a heightened sense of smell. I'm proud to say I didn't vomit once.

The last weed to be collected was nightshade, a vine-like plant with green, teardrop-shaped leaves. "All right," I said as I placed the nightshade in the stuffed container. "We've got the ingredients, and now all we need is the firestone and Harvey." I started to get up when something grabbed my ankle and yanked me off my feet. "Eddie!" I cried out as a vast green and brown vine pulled me into the brush.

"Shelly!" Eddie tried to grab my hand, but I was moving

too fast.

I cursed under my breath in both frustration and amazement as I looked back. The path immediately closed up behind me. I managed to curl up into a ball to protect myself the best I could. Bramble and stones bumped and scraped my arms and legs as I was dragged along the ground. My clothing took a beating, and I could feel blood seeping through the scratches and cuts. At least my husband could follow the scent of my blood. I need to leave a more visible trail for Eddie, I realized. I unclipped my belt and tossed all my weapons aside. Hansel and Gretel left breadcrumbs. I left weapons.

Good thing I did because I was so screwed. The vine snapped up like a whip and flung me towards a cluster of huge Venus flytraps with leaves big enough to swallow an elephant. The jaws of one of the plants opened wide. Its long, green spikes framing the leaves' edges seemed to greedily anticipate its new snack.

I went in headfirst. The gooey substance of the flytrap's stomach enveloped me, and I automatically clamped my mouth shut and plugged my nose. *Oh my god, the prophecy was wrong*, I thought to myself in a panic. *I'm not going to live a thousand years. I'm going to die a slow death being digested by a flesh-eating plant.*

I noticed something sparkling at the stem's base in the plant's stomach acids in the middle of my mental panic attack. *He didn't,* I told myself. Laban had placed the green firestone at the bottom of the flytrap. *That's nasty*, I sighed inwardly. No way was I going to ingest anything poisonous. I swam one-handed down towards the firestone. *Don't vomit, don't vomit* became my mantra. I grabbed it and almost stuffed it into the infinity fanny pack. Not wanting to get any gross plant juices inside the fanny pack, I wisely clutched the gem to my chest.

Now, all I had to do was wait for the plant to slowly digest me. Or die of asphyxiation. Vampires are immortal, but even I can't hold my breath forever. A silver blade penetrated the stem. I backed against the plant as the best I could while the blade sliced it from top to bottom. A familiar hand reached inside and yanked me out.

"Are you okay?" Eddie asked, nonchalantly trying to wipe the plant's stomach acids from his hand.

I let out a long breath and began to cough violently as the fresh, non-acidic air rushed through my lungs. I held up a finger until I finished. "I'm fine now," I assured my husband. "The good news is that I found the firestone!" I produced the gem with a flourish and showed it to him. "It's a little faded, but what do you expect marinating in a giant flesh-eating plant's juices?" I reluctantly unzipped the fanny pack and placed the firestone inside.

"I think we're done here," Eddie said satisfactorily. He had gathered up my weapons and my belt and handed them to me.

"Wait!" Jason said. He peeked his head out of the smallest pocket of the backpack. "What about Harvey?"

"Well, I haven't seen another leprechaun around here, so maybe he's gone," I said, rethreading my belt and clipping the crossbow pistol, Knowledge, and the chakrams back on.

"He also could be hiding anywhere. Neither Shelly nor I sensed anyone else. What is he? Six inches tall?"

Jason looked at us incredulously. "What are you talking about? He's eight-feet tall."

"What?"

"Harvey's not a leprechaun. He's a Green Man."

"Is that a bad rip-off of the Blue Man group?" I asked. I can only read the minds of the undead, but the teenage leprechaun's facial expressions told me precisely what he thought of me. Dumb.

"No, your Majesty. Harvey is a sentient plant being."

I looked around at all the greenery around us. Finding a plant creature in a greenhouse would be like looking for a needle in a stack of needles. I was about to rub my face in aggravation but remembered the drying plant juices on my body. "Okay, we'll look for him," I said. "What does Harvey look like?"

"Have you ever seen *Star Wars*?" Jason asked.

"Are we talking about the original *Star Wars* or the awful prequels?"

"The originals, duh. Anyway, he looks like a plant-version of Chewbacca."

"So, be on the lookout for a green Wookie?" I surmised. I cupped my hands gingerly over my mouth. "Harvey! Harvey!" I called.

No answer.

Eddie and Jason joined in. "Harvey! Harvey!"

Once again, we received no answer.

"He could be scared and hiding," Jason suggested.

"We're being watched," Eddie said as he slowly drew his war scythe.

I followed my husband's lead and drew Knowledge from her sheath. Using my vampire hearing, I concentrated on every sound around us. Something was moving fast to my left. I slashed the vine in two just before it wrapped itself around Eddie's neck. "Jason," I ordered the leprechaun, "in the backpack now!"

"But what if I get crushed?" the teenager asked.

My husband aimed an open palm at Jason. "Citadel!" he said. A green force field enveloped the leprechaun. "Now do as the queen says!" he ordered.

Once Jason was safely inside the backpack, I pressed my back against Eddie's. "How many force fields can you do?" I asked him as I sliced away at another attacking vine.

Another giant flytrap raised its body to its full height and snapped its huge jaws at Eddie. "Just one, babe," he replied as he swung his scythe in a wide arc. The blade found its target and sliced off the flytrap's head.

"Great!" I said as Knowledge slashed through another three vines. "Hendrick was right about these plants. They are definitely evil."

"Or could it be that you and plants don't get along?"

"I didn't kill Robin and Brooke's wedding gift to us!"

"Spider plants aren't supposed to die within a week."

"All right, so I killed that one," I admitted.

Several trees freed themselves from the ground. They used their roots as legs and waded through the mud as if it were water. They drew back their branches. I pressed the underside of my bracelet, and up popped my impenetrable shield, Truth. "Shields up!" I yelled to Eddie as a volley of wooden stakes was thrown at us with an unnerving high speed.

A series of dull THUNKS hit my shield hard enough to knock me off balance. I stumbled backward, and another vine took that opportunity to wrap itself around my shield wrist. I twisted Truth towards me and freed myself with one quick slice.

"Heads up!" Eddie shouted as a colossal oak branch

came swinging at us. We both hit the ground as the branch came within inches of decapitating us. "I think we need a little firefight," my husband said as he dropped his war scythe. Giant balls of white fire appeared over his open palms.

"Hold on! There could be nymphs in those trees. I don't want to hurt them."

"Then what do you suggest?"

"Your energy spell!"

The fire vanished and was replaced by two giant balls of energy. "Duracell!" Eddie shouted as he aimed the balls at the attacking trees. The force of my husband's spell knocked the trees back several hundred feet, conveniently clearing an exit for us. "How's that?" he asked breathlessly. Massive spells like these nearly take the wind out of him.

"Great! How are you doing?"

"Give me a minute," he said, placing his hands on his knees as he gained control of his breathing.

I beheaded three more flytraps who had decided to become mobile. "Now, we both share the honor of being plant killers."

Eddie grabbed the scythe off the ground. "Let's get out of here before the trees get a second wind."

I grabbed his hand. "Good plan," I said as we began to run.

We had to cut our exit short by the time we reached a clearing. A huge green cat was blocking the biodome entrance. Its back was arched in a pouncing position. "I thought the cat was over there," I said, pointing to a vacant spot.

Eddie glanced over his shoulder. "Uh, Shelly, I think the rhinoceros behind us is about to charge," he said. The green rhino was actually snorting at us. We could see leaves blowing up in the air from its nostrils as it lowered its head.

"Actually, rhinos are very gentle creatures, unless they are startled. Then they can charge at speeds of forty-miles-per-hour," I said.

"Unless that piece of obscure information applies to rhinoceros-shaped topiaries, that's not helpful."

"I'm sorry, but that's all I know about them." I looked out of the corner of my eye to see the spinosaurus slowly advancing from our left. "But that's not our only problem."

"What about the three velociraptor topiaries on our right?"

"Crap! We're surrounded by evil topiaries. There is no way I'm going to die!" I said as we pressed our backs against each other.

"Even if we go down gloriously?"

We heard a loud, primal roar and saw a green, human-shaped figure leap onto the cat's back. With one swipe of its long arms, the eight-foot-tall creature took off the cat's head. Then it jumped into the air at the spinosaurus and tore that topiary in half. Eddie and I watched in amazement as it tore apart the raptors and the rhino.

I unzipped the backpack and took out Jason, who was still encased in the force field. "Is that Harvey?" I asked.

The leprechaun's eyes light up in excitement as he nodded. "It is! Harvey! Harvey!" he shouted.

"I think Harvey just saved us," Eddie said.

The Green Man turned and began to slowly advance in our direction. For a moment, his red eyes turned to a gentle, kindly green. Both Eddie and I could smell and see the fresh animal blood all over his mouth. "Or he just eliminated the competition. Uh, Jason, you forget to mention that Harvey was carnivorous."

"No, he's not," Jason said.

"Then why is there blood all over his mouth?" Eddie asked.

"He's a very gentle creature," Jason insisted.

As if to prove our point, a brown bunny ran out in front of Harvey. He violently scooped it up and stuffed it into his mouth. We heard the crunching of bones as blood spilled down his chin.

I looked over at Eddie as we both began mentally calculating the best way to kill the Green Man. "Jason, get back inside," I told the leprechaun as I drew Knowledge.

"He doesn't know what he's doing, your Majesty," Jason argued. "The evilness has affected him. He wouldn't hurt a soul."

"Shelly," Eddie said as he steeled himself for a fight.

"Jason, Harvey's dangerous," I said. "He could kill someone."

"Please, don't hurt him, your Majesty." Tears formed in the teenager's eyes. "Somewhere deep inside is the gentle Harvey.

He's still my friend." Reluctantly he went inside the backpack.

I sighed. I didn't want this kid to lose his friend. I remembered the food in the backpack. Now Harvey was right in front of us. *Eddie put down your weapon*, I mentally told my husband as I slowly slid Knowledge back into her sheath.

What? Are you insane? Eddie asked.

I have a plan to talk him down, but I need you to do as I say.

Eddie warily did as he was asked. *If this plan doesn't work, I'm taking him down.*

Agreed.

"Harvey, we don't want to hurt you," I said, praying my diplomacy skills were as good as I thought they were.

The Green Man snarled at me. He bared his wooden teeth at me.

I remembered a story my dad told me when he was still a police detective. He and his men had cornered a burglar coming off a cocaine high. Dad was talking him down, telling him to put away his tire iron. "We can talk about this," Dad told him, "only if you put down the weapon." Dad put his service weapon away and showed the man his empty hands. "See? I've put away my gun."

"Tell them to put their guns away!" the man screamed.

"Guys," Dad told the three other detectives, "put away your weapons."

"Timothy?" asked Detective Dusty Williams, who was still leveling his weapon at the burglar.

"I can talk him down," Dad had said confidently, "but only if he doesn't perceive us as a threat. Trust me." My father's intuition was correct. The man was arrested without incident after Dad talked him down.

I showed Harvey my hands. "See, Harvey? I'm unarmed. Eddie, show him hands."

The vampire slowly lifted up his hands but kept a wary eye on the plant creature.

"Harvey, I have something for you."

Harvey cocked his head curiously at me.

"Eddie, can you slowly take off your backpack?" I asked calmly.

"Sure," my husband said. He slowly shrugged off the

backpack and placed it on the ground. *Now what?*

Trust me.

I do, but I'm not letting my guard down.

I know. I unhurriedly unzipped the back zipper. "I've got a present for you in here, Harvey. I think you'll like it." I casually reached inside and put out a can of Vienna sausages. I showed Harvey the can. "Do you know what's in here, Harvey? Little wiener dogs. They're perfect for you. No fur or bones." I pulled open the tab and did something incredibly dangerous and stupid at the same time. I waved the can under the Green Man's nose.

Apparently, canned meat was very alluring to him because he greedily tried to grab it and nearly took my hand with him.

I drew the sausages close to my chest. "No, Harvey, you can't have the entire can."

He roared angrily and was about to take off my head when I pulled out one of the sausages and tossed it to him. He caught it and sniffed it cautiously before stuffing it into his mouth. A green tongue appeared as he ran it around his mouth in satisfaction.

"Delicious, isn't it?" I asked. "Do you want another one?"

Harvey nodded enthusiastically and caught the next sausage I threw in his mouth. What I took for a smile spread across his lips. He pointed to the can and held out his hand. His red eyes were slowly changing back to a gentle green.

"I'll give you some more, but you've got to promise not to hurt us. Can you do that, Harvey?"

He nodded like a happy Labrador retriever. A Labrador who had just swallowed a bunny whole. He pointed to the exit.

"Do you want to leave here, Harvey?" I asked as I tossed him another one.

Another enthusiastic nod as he gobbled it up.

"If you leave, you can't hurt people or animals," I said.

He pointed to the backpack and clapped his hands excitedly.

"What's he doing, Shelly?" Eddie asked hesitantly.

"I don't know. Let me try something. Harvey, do you want to say hi to Jason?"

At the mention of the leprechaun's name, Harvey began to jump up and down like a little kid who just got a pony for

Christmas. I let Jason out, and the Green Man began to make happy noises.

"What did you do?" Jason asked me, his voice full of astonishment.

"The queen just used Vienna sausages as a part of a diplomatic process," Eddie said, conveying both shock and admiration.

Back at Castle DeLorean, the Shortstalk clan and Harvey were settling into the royal gardens. Eddie and I realized the only way to keep Harvey from going evil was to feed him the little sausages, and the leprechauns refused to leave him alone. I made the executive decision to have all of them live in the royal gardens where we could continue to feed the Green Man my inherited lifetime supply of cocktail wieners. I gave Gunther the flowers and the firestone. Then my husband and I took showers and changed our clothes before our next quest.

Chapter Eleven:
Taking the "Fun" Out of Funhouse

"Wow, another creepy place Hiram has sent us to," Eddie said as we surveyed our surroundings.

"I don't know, Eddie. I'm sure this place was trendy in its time." I stared up at the rusted wrought iron sign that hung precariously above us in the twenty-foot arching gate. Every other letter of the Boulle Family Fairgrounds threatened to break loose with the slightest bit of wind.

Eddie scratched some fading red paint off the side of the gate. "Not anymore. Gunther says this place has been abandoned since the Demon Wars."

"Really sad," I said. "I bet a lot of families had some happy memories here." I thought about the economy of my queendom. On the outside, the city seemed grandiose, but the people were unhappy. The Demon Wars really hurt Peregrin. "War sucks," I said.

Eddie jumped the rusted turnstile. "What?"

"I was just thinking about how the Demon Wars really affected Peregrin. I never want to drive this country into war."

"What would you do if it ever happened?"

I jumped the turnstile to join my husband on the other side. "First, I would try to avoid war as much as I could."

"And if you couldn't?"

"If all diplomatic efforts failed, then war would be a very last resort."

"If war ever comes, I know you'll do the right thing."

"This is why I married you because you'll always have my back. I might need my back if we find the rest of these firestones." I glanced at the GPS on Eddie's phone. "So, where exactly is the firestone this time?"

He glanced at the screen. "About thirty yards straight ahead," he estimated.

"Lead on!" I said as I took his hand. As we walked, I took in the sights. Even though the midway was abandoned, I was surprised with how clean it was. Not a piece of trash in sight.

"There has to be someone here. Look how clean this place is. We could eat off the ground without plates."

Eddie turned and gave me a disgusted look. "Eww."

"I said 'could,' honey," I said. "Not that I would ever eat off the ground where hundreds of people walked in with who knows what."

"Good," he said, "because I was starting to think you'd lost it with all these insane quests."

"No, but I'm dancing on edge." My stomach rumbled to remind me we hadn't eaten since breakfast. It was well past lunchtime. "Man, I wish I had a funnel cake right now. Loaded with two inches of powdered sugar. I could also go for a big stick of cotton candy."

Eddie looked like he was about to throw up. "That's disgusting."

I was shocked. "How can you object to carnival food? Your sweet tooth is worse than mine."

"I don't eat carnival food."

"Why not?"

"When I worked as a ride mechanic at a carnival one

summer, I saw what they put in the food."

"What?"

"The powdered sugar on the funnel cake was not sugar."

"Heroin?"

"No, baby powder."

"That's nasty!"

"You know what they dropped in the cotton candy machine?"

"I'm afraid to ask."

"Cigarette butts."

"That's nastier and a health hazard! Thanks, hon, now you've turned me off carnival food forever."

Eddie kissed me. "Consider it a public service, babe."

I unzipped the front of his backpack and searched for something to eat. I grabbed a couple of apples, handed one to Eddie, and I took a bite out of mine. "You know what this apple needs?"

Eddie swallowed the bite of his apple. "To be smothered in caramel?"

"Did you just read my mind?" I asked my husband.

"No, I just know you," he replied. He looked down at his phone and then up at a one-story building with fading colors in swirling patterns. The word "funhouse" arched over a giant clown's laughing mouth. "I think the firestone is somewhere in here."

"Fantastic! I've never been in a funhouse," I said.

Eddie dug our headlamps out of his backpack and tossed one to me. "I think we're going to need these," he said as he turned on his.

"Well, the good thing is that this place is abandoned, so we should have no problem getting the firestone," I said as I walked through the clown's mouth.

The moment we entered, bright interior lights flashed on, nearly blinding me. Circus music began to play loudly overhead as a prerecorded voice boomed across the entrance. "Welcome to Bubble's Funhouse, where every step you take is a step towards fun!"

Fumbling in search of my headlamp's off switch, I shouted to Eddie over the loud noise. "I thought this place was supposed to be abandoned."

"It must have motion sensors. The newer models have them installed for upgrade purposes."

Or employee laziness, I thought to myself. I stepped into a six-foot-tall wide tunnel lined with glow-in-the-dark stars and planets. I could see a door at least twenty-feet ahead of me. I began to walk across the tunnel when it suddenly began to spin. I lost my balance and fell to the floor.

"You o—Whoa!" A loud thump came from behind me.

"Careful, honey!" I said as I slowly got to my feet.

"Ow! I think I broke something. Like my spleen."

I glanced at my husband, who was flat on his back. "I'm pretty sure breaking a spleen is physically impossible."

He scrambled to his feet and touched his back. "Whatever. My vampire healing is repairing my broken spleen."

I declined to comment as I tried to walk steadily. Then the tunnel floor shifted counter-clockwise violently under our feet. We collided with each other and fell back on the ground. "Walking is not going to be an option here," I said.

"Crawling it is then," Eddie remarked as we started to

make our way to the door.

I wasn't watching my hands because I concentrated on the rotating that was causing my head to spin. "Oh, gross! I'm pretty sure I've discovered some fresh animal droppings."

"Please, don't say that. I'm trying not to vomit right now. This tunnel is making me nauseous."

"Sorry," I apologized. We finally made it to the door, which creaked open on its own.

Once we were inside, we stood up shakily, attempting to regain our balance and sense of direction. This wasn't the least bit helped by the several disco balls that suddenly flickered to life and began to spin around, casting shards of bright light everywhere.

"Stupid funhouse trying to blind us," I muttered as I walked forward and smacked right into a mirror. I forgot: Funhouses usually had mirror mazes but no two street-smart vampires.

I heard Eddie curse under his breath as he, too, walked into a mirror. Maze: One, vampires: Zero. "You'd think that these kinds of mazes would have no effect on us."

"It's this stupid disco ball. It's disorienting us. At least it's not strobe lights." Just as the words came from my mouth, we were enveloped into total darkness for a few moments until several blinding strobe lights emanated from the disco balls.

"You just had to say that, Shelly, didn't you?"

"Crap! We need a plan if we're going to make it out of here with our sight intact."

Eddie caught me glancing at him. "Why are you looking at me?" he asked. "You're the one who usually comes up with the plans."

"Because you're the carnival expert."

"Working one summer as a ride mechanic doesn't make me an expert."

I pulled out my crossbow pistol. "Yes, it does. I've only been to carnivals as a guest." I took aim at where I thought one of the strobe lights was located and pulled the trigger. The arrow flew out into the darkness and hit something which clearly wasn't my target. "Strobe lights don't squeal, do they?"

"Not usually. What did you hit?"

"Definitely not the strobe light." I quickly put away the crossbow pistol. "Maybe I shouldn't be firing blindly in here."

"Ya think?" Eddie pulled out his war scythe and extended it to its full length. "Come on, Tex. I know how to get out of here." Using the scythe like a blind person's cane, my husband and I began to navigate the maze. "You see, the trick is to keep something touching the wall at all times." The insistent tapping on the mirrors told us where the walls were. Either that or he was doing it to annoy me.

We were about a minute into the navigation when I saw a rabbit-shaped thing with a noticeable limp scurrying along the tops of the seven-foot-tall mirrors when in the blink of a strobe light. "What the heck was that?" I said, grabbing Eddie's hand.

He stopped. "What?"

"I saw something on top of the mirrors." I pointed to where I had seen the thing.

With the help of the blinding strobe light, he attempted to scan the tops of the mirrors. "I don't see anything. What did it look like?"

"Rabbity, definitely rabbity, but with a long thin tail."

"Was it bleeding yellow?"

"I don't know. Why?"

Eddie pointed to streaks of dripping yellow blood lining the tops of the mirrors. "I think we've found your elusive target."

"We should follow it. It could lead us to the exit."

"You took the words right out of my mouth, Shell."

"Let's follow the yellow blood road!"

Unlike Dorothy and her pals, Eddie and mine's yellow brick road went dead cold, quite literally, about two minutes later. We followed the bloody mirrors, sans skipping and singing until we came across the source of the blood. Curled up in the death position was the weirdest thing we had ever seen. It had the head of a rabbit and legs and a long thin tail. My arrow was sticking out of its rat-shaped body. "What is it?" I asked Eddie.

"Don't know. I've never seen anything like it before." He poked it with the end of the war scythe.

"What are you doing?"

"I'm seeing if it's really dead."

"Don't you watch horror movies? That's one of the cardinal rules of survival: Don't poke dead things with a stick."

"I thought one of the cardinal rules was not having

teenage sex."

"That's one of the rules, too."

"Well, it's definitely dead," Eddie said as he swept it to the side of our path. "Come on. We should be near the exit." We started back on our way.

"Do you think that's the only one in here?"

"Well, based on my knowledge of rat and rabbit biology, I'm going to say no."

A shiver ran up my spine. I hated rodents. The last thing I wanted was more of these creepy science experiments from hell running across my feet. My mind drifted back to the time I had unfortunately discovered a rats' nest in my basement. I was thirteen at the time and was totally creeped out. My dad shared these great words of wisdom when I was too terrified to do laundry. "They're more scared of you than you are of them," he had told me. Which, by no means, will comfort a teenager who had just stumbled across the rats hanging out in a pile of her family's clothes. "Puppies and rainbows, puppies and rainbows," I began to repeat aloud in a failing attempt to rid my mind of the creepy rodent thing.

"What's up with the 'puppies and rainbows" mantra?" Eddie asked.

I stopped. "It's my new mantra to rid my mind of gross things."

"How's it working?"

"You know what we just saw? A puppy and a rainbow!"

"Great, my wife is in denial," Eddie joked.

"You have your coping mechanisms. I have mine."

Suddenly the mirror next to me began to fall. My husband dropped Vengeance, grabbed me, and pulled me close to him as he evoked his force shield spell. Shards of glass splintered around the outside of the green ball of protective energy as every single mirror in the maze toppled over in a deafening cacophony. To make matters worse, every single light went out, casting us into utter darkness. We waited for a few minutes for the lights to come back on. We both knew how dangerous it was to wade through broken glass in the dark.

Eddie dismissed the spell, and the energy vanished. He reached into his backpack and pulled out our headlamps. As the vampire turned his headlamp on, he surveyed the damage while searching for his war scythe. "Exit's over there," he said, indicating a door with an old emergency exit sign hanging above. "Old amusement park falling apart, right?" he asked as he found Vengeance. He picked up the scythe and converted it back to the size of a billy club.

"Or maybe it was karma for you poking the dead rodent thing. I told you not to poke it."

"If this is karma, it's biting you, too. You shot the thing." He took my hand as we began to gingerly navigate our way to the exit.

"Let's just say it was a freak accident and leave it at that."

"Sounds good to me."

We made it to safety with only glass in the soles of our sneakers. Once we stepped over the threshold, we barely had time to breathe a sigh of relief. The floor opened under our feet, and we found ourselves whipping through a winding plastic tunnel slide faster than the speed of light. The inside was painted in glow-in-the-dark psychedelic colors that made me want to vomit every rainbow color.

We finally landed in a ten-foot-tall cage reinforced with netting on all sides. Fortunately, our landing was not so soft due to the four-foot-high pile of harden, multi-colored balls, which time had not been kind to. I gave a moan of pain.

"You okay, Shelly?" Eddie asked.

"Yep, I'm just going to lie here for an indefinite period of time."

Eddie waded through the balls and attempted to help me up, but we both tripped on the balls under our feet. We lay there staring up at the slide, silently taunting us from on high. "If we didn't have these balls, I think we could jump to reach the slide."

"I think they might have a different idea," I said, pointing to the dozens of the rodent-things that had begun to scale the netting. I attempted to withdraw Knowledge, but I soon discovered it is tough to unsheathe a sword in a ball pit.

"Let's just hope these guys are herbivorous."

We didn't have any time to find out because the entire cage was hit with a huge electronic pulse. Before we passed out, we heard a rich, Cajun accent say, "Blasted gremlins!"

My head was spinning when I woke up. I tried to sit up, but a hand pushed me back on the cot. "Careful, cher," an unfamiliar voice told me. "You just got quite a shock."

"Well, of course, we did. You electrocuted us," I heard my husband say dryly. "How are you feeling, Shell?"

"Like I've touched an electric fence." I slowly sat up and finally got a good look at my surroundings. We were in a tiny, compact kitchen inside of what looked like the cab of a truck. We were in someone's RV.

A chimpanzee wearing a plaid shirt and overalls handed me a cup. "Drink this, cher. It'll help with your head," he said.

I hesitantly took a sip, almost forgot my manners as I nearly spit it out. "What the heck is that?"

The ape laughed heartily. "I never said it tasted good, but my pawpaw's mushroom tea can cure anything. Allow me to introduce myself, Jean-Claude Bolle, at your service."

I set the cup down and shook his hand. "Shelly Van Helsing, and I see you've already met my husband, Eddie," I said.

"Mr. Bolle has been having trouble with gremlins for over a

year," Eddie explained. "He thought they were in the ball pit again."

"Mr. Bolle was my father, but you can call me Jean-Claude. Those nasty critters have taken over my family's property, and I can't seem to keep on top of them."

"The rodent-things are gremlins?" I asked.

Jean-Claude nodded. "They are very destructive, and I can't have them here when I open up the carnival. I heard that Peregrin's got a new queen who is supposed to be better than Queen Rachel."

I looked over at Eddie. *He doesn't know who we are, does he?* I asked telepathically.

I certainly didn't mention it, he replied.

I considered the next words from my mouth carefully. "So, what was wrong with Queen Rachel?"

"She was nothing but a cold-blooded murderer; let me tell you, cher. She ordered a public execution of the entire sheriff's office and their families. Public execution, my foot. It was more like a slaughter. Her guardian killed every single one of them without even a second glance. Even little kids."

I could barely contain my horrified shock at this news. "Why?"

"Because Diamondback was being investigated for dragging people from their homes and accusing them of being morally wrong. Sometimes he would publically kill them."

"What do you mean by 'morally wrong'?" I asked.

"For having a different way of life which the queen and the Minister of Virtue disagreed with. My pa was the sheriff, and I was a young deputy, and Pa informed Queen Rachel of her Guardian's actions. When the queen ordered a public execution of the department, my father told me to come here. Those were the last words he ever said to me. She put a bounty on my head, but now with the new queen, I hope it will be revoked."

"Did Queen Rachel ever do anything good for the queendom?" I asked.

"Not to my knowledge, she caused a lot of heartache and grief to an already hurting country."

"So my sister was always evil," I replied.

A look of horror crossed Jean-Claude's face. "You're the new queen?" he asked. He got down on his hands and knees and began to grovel at my feet. "Please forgive me, your Majesty. I spoke ill of your sister."

"Believe me, I speak ill of her all the time," I said. "Don't be afraid. I'm not going to punish you or anything. Actually, we might be able to help each other out."

Jean-Claude got up with a relieved but quizzical look on his face. "How so?" he asked suspiciously.

"We help you with your gremlin problem, and you can help us find this gemstone."

"And how do you propose to do that?" the chimpanzee asked.

I thought about it for a moment. "What have you tried?"

"Poisons, rodent bombs, and even shooting them with my pulse gun. The gun would temporarily scare them off."

I had a sudden thought. When we had the rats in the basement, Dad bought several ultrasonic rodent repellents. The rats left within hours. "Could you rig up a few ultrasonic repellents and place them near the gremlins' nests?"

"That might work," Jean-Claude answered.

"Yeah, I could help you rig some up in an hour," Eddie

offered.

"Let's give it a shot," Jean-Claude answered.

While the men worked on their DIY rodent repellents, I slept in the RV. Terrifying images of families and lovers being slaughtered while my sister looked on in approval haunted my dreams. I could see people huddling in fear in their own houses. I awoke with a start. The vision was more confirmation I needed to restore Peregrin to a country where no one would live in fear of his or her government. Eddie and Jean-Claude returned to the RV with satisfied grins.

"It worked perfectly, Shelly," my husband told me.

"Yep, them varmints ran like they'd been dosed with ghost peppers. I've never seen anything like it." Jean-Claude said excitedly. "I think I know where your gemstone is."

Jean-Claude led us back to the funhouse, which surprisingly had a huge basement carved deep into the ground. On the floor was a ginormous piano atop of several giant gears. "One of my pawpaw's employees wanted to install this Piano of Doom, but Pawpaw deemed it unsafe. The rascal told my pawpaw that this challenge's object was to play 'Mary had a Little Lamb' on the keyboard. But one misstep could mean your doom."

"Meaning what?" Eddie asked.

"The wrong keys would crumble beneath you."

I peered at the metal gears as an unpleasant image of someone getting crushed by them formed in my mind. "That would be a nasty end." In the middle of the keyboard was a bright pink firestone. "And our quarry." Without thinking, I jumped onto the first key, which crumbled beneath my feet. I let out a shriek as I started to fall before I grabbed the shattered wooden edge.

With lightning speed, Eddie whipped out Vengeance and extended it to its full length. He lay flat on his stomach and pointed the end towards me. "Grab on!"

I reached for the war scythe with my free hand as my other arm screamed in protest. My fingers barely brushed against Vengeance. "I can't reach it!" I said through clenched teeth. I looked up, and to my horror, a menacing bunny face peered down at me. "I thought you guys got rid of the gremlins!"

"We did!" Jean-Claude replied.

"Then what the heck is that?" I shouted.

Eddie pulled his Scorpion XL from his ankle holster and fired a deadly shot at the gremlin. Its head exploded, showering me with blood and brain matter. Gross. Glancing down, I saw the gears beneath me come to life. Crap! Gremlins weren't going to kill me. The fall would. I gripped the edge with both hands and hoisted myself onto the keyboard. Fortunately, it didn't break.

"Are you okay, Shelly?" Eddie asked as he readied himself to jump to my rescue. "I'm coming over."

"No, don't. I don't think the keyboard could support both our weight."

"I would recommend that you play 'Mary had a Little Lamb,' your Majesty," Jean-Claude suggested. "Are you musically inclined?"

"I can play the radio," I answered.

Jean-Claude gave a disappointed shake of his head. "Your Majesty, is this gemstone worth your life?" he asked.

"He's got a point, babe," Eddie said.

I was about to make a fantastic comeback when my eyes

began to cloud as dizziness and nausea swept over me. *Crap, just what I need. A vision*, I thought before my mind went to another time and place.

Mom sits at the piano with me and cringes as I butcher the music piece. "Shelly, stop and let me show you again," she says.

I stop playing and watch in absolute amazement as my talented mother's fingers dance on the black and white keys, eloquently playing "Mary Had a Little Lamb." "How come I can't play like you?" I ask her after she is done playing. "I've been practicing for years, Mom, and I still can't get the simplest tunes. Robin plays almost as well as you do, and he's only a year older than I am. Everyone in the family can play a musical instrument, except for me. Dad plays the guitar, you play the piano, and Robin plays both the piano and the violin. I just wish I could be musical like everyone else."

"Shelly, one day, you will become someone very important."

"Like the president?"

Mom only smiles as she begins to play the familiar nursery rhyme. "Something like that."

I lean against her, the familiar, comforting smell of her strawberry-vanilla perfume surrounding me. The simple tune lulled me into . . .

BANG! A shot brought me out of my vision. Yellow gremlin blood splattered all over me. "We really need to rethink your pest control methods!" I shouted to Jean-Claude.

"You okay, Shell?" Eddie asked as he fired another shot at a gremlin who was leaping in mid-air.

"Yeah, I'm fine." Another shot rang in my ear. "Just stop shooting. I need to concentrate."

"Concentrate on what?" Jean-Claude asked as he let loose a volley of electrical pulses at a small group of gremlins who were climbing on top of shifting gears. Geesh, these creatures must breed like rabbits.

"I need to remember the music notes in the correct order to get the firestone." I thought about the notes Mom played in my vision. The first note was B. I jumped to it, and the key was stable. "A!" I sang out as I jumped to the second note. Same result. "G-A-B-B-A-A-A-B-D-D-B-A-G-A-B-B-B-A-A-B-A-G." I sang aloud each note at the top of my lungs as I jumped gracefully from key to key. Gremlins scattered from my presence. I would like to think it was because Eddie and Jean-Claude were blowing them to pieces, but now I realize it was because of my singing.

The last key landed me right below the firestone. I leaped up next to the pink gemstone, grabbed it triumphantly, and held it above my head. "Veni! Vidi! Vici!" I shouted.

Apparently, the firestone was holding the entire piano together. Don't ask me how. The wood crumbled beneath my feet, and I felt myself falling headlong into the grinding gears. Yes, I did clutch the firestone to my chest as if it were my baby.

Eddie suddenly swung by and grabbed my waist before I fell to my death.

" Na na na na na na na na na na na na na na na na Batmaaan!" He sang out as we swung to the other side of the pit. When he saw the piano start to crumble, he had whipped out his grappling gun and shot the steel cable into the opposite. Like the caped crusader, he swung across the gap and rescued me from certain death.

We landed safely on the other side. "You've always wanted to say that, haven't you?" I asked him.

"Even more since I got this awesome grappling gun," Eddie said with a huge grin. "You okay?"

I peered at the crumbled keyboard being crushed by the gears. "Better than the piano," I said as I turned and kissed the vampire. "Nice job, Batman."

"Are you all right, your Majesties?" Jean-Claude shouted to us.

"We're fine!" Eddie assured him. He looked at me. "You had another vision, didn't you?"

I nodded with a smile. "For once, it was a nice one. I saw my mom, and she helped me play the right tune." I told him about the vision.

Eddie grinned. Whenever I talk about my late mother, there was always a hint of sadness in my voice. So to see me smile now really lifted his heart. "So she hinted about you becoming queen."

I nodded and was silent for a moment. "Six firestones down, one more to go."

We spent the next couple of hours helping Jean-Claude get rid of the gremlins. He and Eddie had to increase the wattage of the electromagnetic pulse. I stayed safely away. I'm not too fond of being electrocuted. The chimpanzee was so grateful for our assistance that he decided to reopen the amusement park. "I'm going to give you annual passes," he told us.

Chapter Twelve:
If I Only Had a Brain,
Along with a Few Other Vital Organs

The last quest was no doubt the worst and the most dangerous one. The Monte Carlo crew dropped Eddie and me off at the edge of a large, flat, barren island on the fringes of the queendom. The only thing on the land was a huge, black dome covering almost thirty acres. The top of the dome was at least eight stories high. "Wow! Domes in Peregrin are very trendy," my husband observed.

"I know! I've never seen so many domes in my entire life." I craned my neck up as much as I could without giving myself whiplash. "Wonder what horrors we are going to encounter in here?"

"Maybe we'll be lucky, and the next quest will be a walk in

the park." Eddie put out his cell phone and plugged in the firestone's coordinates. "We've got a good hike ahead of us. You ready?"

I glanced around the dome, searching for a way in. I couldn't tell if the structure was made out of tinted glass or black marble plates. I picked up a rock and tossed it at the dome. It made a tinkling sound.

"What was that for?" Eddie asked.

"Just testing to see what the dome was made of. It's made of glass."

"Didn't you tell me not to test things on unknown objects?"

"Yeah, but you couldn't see the mechanical squirrels at Dr. Wandasen's tree. I can see the top of the dome, and there is no danger at all."

"Then what about the sign on this door?" Eddie pointed to a door the same color as the rest of the dome. Even the hinges were painted to hide the door in plain sight. He had wiped away the dirt on the sign, which read: DANGER: DO NOT ENTER. "I think we just jinxed ourselves," he said as he ripped the padlock off its chain.

"Yet we are going in," I replied.

"We can't give up this far in the quest." Eddie pushed open the door, and we entered.

The moonlight barely penetrated through the dome's structure, peppering the enormous interior with spots of light, but that wasn't giving off the eerie, green glow. "I'm pretty sure corn isn't supposed to glow neon-green like that," I observed as I stared up at the fifteen-foot corn stalks.

"What kind of fertilizer did this guy use?"

"Glow sticks?" I guessed. I spotted a conveniently trimmed path to our left. "Off we go."

We entered the left and began to walk along a twisting, debris-free path. A few minutes later, Eddie looked down at his phone in frustration. "What is wrong with this thing?"

We stopped, and I looked down at the phone with him. "Why is it saying 'recalculating'? Did we miss a turn somewhere?"

Eddie looked around at the stalks towering over us. "I think we're in a corn maze. The incredibly clean paths are a huge indicator."

"Then who is taking care of it? Gunther said this place was abandoned." I asked.

"Don't know, but living near this chemically enhanced corn can't be doing anyone anything good, health-wise. Ah, screw it." Eddie said after his GPS informed him that it was recalculating again. He slipped his phone into his backpack. "Let's go find that farmhouse porch.

We began weaving our way through the twisting maze and hadn't got very far when I spotted a twenty-foot tall figure hanging from a thirty-foot, T-shaped pole. I realized it was a scarecrow, a scary-looking one at that. The face looked like dry skin with big, black button eyes. Its mouth was painted blood red with the painted-on triangle nose. It was dressed in a faded, plaid shirt with straw sticking out from his collar. Instead of straw-filled gloves, it had rakes for hands with sharp metal prongs. Its overalls had red splotches on the front. "Why would someone have a scarecrow in a dome-covered cornfield?" I asked.

"Covering a cornfield in a dome does defeat the purpose of scarecrows," Eddie replied.

"That scarecrow is very creepy," I said with a sudden urge to keep moving at a fast pace.

My husband noticed the apprehension in my voice and gave my hand a reassuring squeeze. "Let's keep moving."

We started the navigation again and encountered six more scarecrows in the scary field. Fortunately, seeing them wasn't the most terrifying thing. It was when we could no longer see them.

The sudden movement in the stalks alerted me to the danger. I looked up at the bare poles. "Eddie," I whispered. "Where are the scarecrows?"

The vampire looked at me with concern. He drew Vengeance to its full, deadly length. "Stay close. I think things are about to get dangerous."

I kept my hand on Knowledge's hilt. "Don't worry about me. I've seen enough horror movies to know not to wander off."

"I think our best bet is to find the firestone and get out of here."

I was about to agree when two huge, shadowy figures lept out in front of us, blocking our path. The scarecrows were much scarier up close with their unhinged jaws and multiple rows of razor-sharp teeth. I realized the red splotches on their overalls were not paint but fresh blood. I turned around to see two more scarecrows behind us. "Honey, we've got two more behind us," I said, masking my terror with calmness. I slowly drew my sword and activated my shield bracelet as my husband, and I pressed our backs against each other.

"I think we can take them," Eddie said. "They're just dumb scarecrows, right?"

He was wrong. They opened their mouths and spoke in unison. "Yum, yum! Fleshy, fleshy maze runners!" They jumped at us.

"Okay, I take it back," Eddie said as he activated his own shield bracelet. "They're not dumb." He swung Vengeance and took off one of the heads.

One of the scarecrows jumped at me. I threw up my shield to protect myself, and the strawman hit it hard. I heard something crack inside my arm, and I dropped Knowledge as I gasped in pain.

With lightning speed, Eddie whipped around. "Duracell!"

he shouted as two large, blue balls of energy appeared in his palms. He threw them at the scarecrows and quickly took out both. Their straw limbs exploded from their bodies "You okay, Shell?"

"I think my arm's broken," I replied through clenched teeth. "I just need time to heal." I could already feel the bones repair themselves.

"How much time?"

"Would five or ten minutes give me enough healing time?"

"I don't know. It takes me only a few moments, but I've been a vampire a lot longer than you have. I can give you some time." He placed one hand on my shoulder and outstretched the other as he shouted, "Citadel!" Instantly, a green force field surrounded us.

"Heal faster," I whispered to my broken arm. I looked up through the green haze and saw that the scarecrows whom Eddie had decapitated were putting their heads back on as if nothing happened. The other scarecrows were putting their limbs back together. "Don't think dismemberment is going to get rid of these guys."

"Fire will get rid of them."

"No," I said, reading my husband's mind. "No more spells. The more you use, the more you lose your energy, and we can't risk that."

"I have a plan."

"Please, tell me it's a good one."

"Remember my plan at the roc's nest?"

I remembered. "That's a terrible plan."

"It's our only option. We—."

I put up a hand to silence my husband as I noticed all four scarecrows cocking their heads like dogs. *I think they can hear and understand us*, I said telepathically.

Great. Have you ever gone through a corn maze?

I did once with Robin, Roger, and Lisa when we were in high school. Don't ever let my brother lead you through a maze. It took us two-and-half hours before we got out.

When I was training with the Agency, they had me run through one. We just have to keep to the left.

How long did it take you?

Ten minutes, then again, I wasn't being hunted down by

flesh-eating scarecrows. How's your arm?

I wiggled my fingers without pain. Perfectly healed.

Eddie took my hand. *Ready?* When I nodded in response,

he dismantled the force field. "Run!"

We did as fast as we could, weaving through the

complicated maze. Stalks slapped against our faces and limbs

as we dodged our pursuers. The scarecrows were gaining on us.

The stalks moved ominously in the dome's eerie light. I felt like

one of those poor extras in the Lost World movie who were going

to get unsuspectedly eaten by the velociraptors hiding in the tall

grass. At least the raptors weren't chanting, "Yum, yum. Fleshy,

fleshy maze runners," in coordination with the old Hide-and-Seek

mantra, "Come out, come out wherever you are."

Eddie and I turned a corner, and a clawed arm swiped at

my husband's leg. He collapsed to the ground in pain as blood

began to leak out of a large gash in his calf.

"Eddie, can you get up?"

He struggled to his feet as he tried to stand up using his

war scythe. "I'm fine," he lied. "Let's keep going."

"Uh, no, you're not," I said. "The back of your leg is

bleeding."

"It's just a scratch," he said through clenched teeth. "I can walk." He attempted to prove it to me by taking a few steps, but he fell to his knees. "Okay, maybe a muscle got torn," he admitted. "But we've got to keep moving. Those things are hunting us."

"I've got an idea." Without giving my husband a chance to ask, I closed my eyes and willed myself to transform. Opening my eyes, I was enveloped into a mist of gold and black sparkles as my body began to morph into a sleek black panther. I motioned for Eddie to climb on my back.

"So, can you talk in your panther form?" he asked once he was secure.

I wasn't sure to open my mouth to speak, but only a low growl came out. Maybe telepathy would work. *I can't talk in this form, but I can still telecommunicate with you.*

Let's get going, Eddie said as he wrapped his legs around my body and his arms around my neck.

Don't even think about calling me Kitty, I warned him as I broke into a run. As a vampire, I was fast, but I was running at over fifty miles per hour when I was in my black panther form. Leaving corn stalks in my wake, I followed Eddie's mental instructions as I navigated the rest of the maze.

The coolest part was when one of the scarecrows stepped out in front of us. I didn't even slow down. Instead, I jumped over it, barely clearing its head. I landed on my feet and resumed my running like the coolest cat in the world.

That was amazing! Forget turning into mist. You've got the best transformation I've ever seen.

Awe! Thanks, honey. I looked up to see a dilapidated barn about thirty yards ahead of us. The building was red once, but now time and most likely, radiation had turned into a rusty brown color. Two gray doors flanked a big, gray garage door.

I think the firestone's in there.

Good, because I'm getting exhausted. My body was slowing down. If I didn't change soon, I wouldn't make it. *How's your leg?*

Healed completely.

We had just reached the barn when one of the doors swung open by itself into darkness. I glanced over my shoulder and saw the scarecrows at our heels. I had to make a split-second decision: Enter the door into darkness or get ripped apart by flesh-eating scarecrows.

It didn't take a rocket scientist to figure it out. I bounded into the dark barn and went into an uncontrollable skid. My claws tried to find traction, but I couldn't see a blessed thing. Then we smacked into something wooden. Eddie was thrown off my back, and I lay motionless in a heap as I felt my panther form morph back into my fully clothed vampire self.

Then the barn was bathed in bright light. I shut my eyes, not from pain (I had the wind knocked out of me) but to let them adjust to the sudden brightness. "Shelly, are you okay?" Eddie asked as I heard him crouch down next to me.

"I think so. You?"

"I'm okay." He helped me to my feet. "I think you ran into these barrels." He pointed to an open barrel on its side. Clear liquid ran out of it. He took a sniff. "I think that's moonshine."

I looked around. Aside from the barrel mess, the entire barn was spic and span. Even the large, old tractor in the corner was gleaning in the light. I glanced at the door we had come through. To my shock, it was shut. A long two-by-four had been placed across it to prevent anyone else from coming through.

"Eddie, did you close the door and turn on the lights?"

Eddie looked at the door and then at me. "I thought you did it with your cool, panther powers."

"No. Why would I have powers to flick on a light switch and barricade a door?"

My husband shrugged. "I don't know."

"I did, and you're trespassing!" shouted a voice above us.

We looked up to see a yellow and black basketball-size Koosh ball leap down from an open loft. I reached up and caught it. "Koosh balls? Seriously, you're going to have to do better than that!" I yelled up to the loft. "The eighties called. They want their toy back."

"Who are you calling a toy?" the thing in my hands snarled.

"Ahh!" I instinctively threw it to the ground.

The thing rolled a couple of feet, and hands and legs popped out of it. Then a head with yellow and black hair appeared, and two angry eyes glared at me. "Is that any way to treat a brownie?"

I blinked in confusion. "I'm sorry. I've never seen a brownie before."

"I ain't no toy either!"

"Sorry," I apologized again. "We thought this farm was abandoned."

"Does it look abandoned to you numbskulls?" the brownie snapped.

I was going to tell him not to insult the king and queen, but I let it slide, considering I had called him an eighties toy. "We got off on the wrong foot. I'm Shelly Van Helsing, and this is my husband, Eddie. You are?"

The brownie crossed his arms angrily. "Fagin. I was the assistant to Farmer Swenson, the wizard who lived here."

"Is he the one responsible for those cannibalistic scarecrows?" Eddie asked Fagin.

"They weren't like that at first."

"The scarecrows were nice, flesh-eating creatures?" I asked incredulously.

"Of course not!" Fagin said irritably.

"I'm confused," I said.

"Ever since that firestone showed up, the scarecrows turned from simple strawmen to those things."

"Are you saying the firestone did this? Are we going to turn into horrible mutant creatures?" I asked.

Fagin put his face in his palm and mumbled something about idiotic vampires. "Firestones are only radioactive if you are stupid enough to dabble in black magic!"

Okay, someone was not a happy camper. "I take it Farmer Swenson did just that," Eddie guessed.

"He was a young Welkie farmer who wanted to make sure the queendom would buy corn only from his fields. So when he found the firestone, his greedy little mind decided to draw black magic from the firestone."

I looked around for the telltale sign of black magic. That's when I spotted it. Part of a painted black circle was hidden under the back wheels of the red tractor. Squatting down, I could make out the rest of the sign painted on the barn's floor. Inside the circle was a black hand with a lightning bolt across the open palm. Streaks of red had been smeared across the circle. "What is this?" I asked, pointing to the red lines.

"Chicken blood," Fagin said. "Farmer Swenson was a greedy man, but not a killer."

"No, he left that to his flesh-eating scarecrows," Eddie said. "What happened to him?"

"They turned on him one night and took his skin as a trophy," Fagin said.

"That's horrible. I'm so sorry that you lost your friend."

The brownie laughed. "A friend? He treated me like a servant, nothing more. I had been in his family service for decades. When those creatures ripped him apart, my heart was filled with gladness."

Eddie and I exchanged surprised glances. Okay, we were chatting with a very angry and quite possible sociopathic brownie who could probably kill both of us without a care in the world. I decided to use my diplomatic charm on him. "What if we took care of both the firestone and the evil scarecrows?"

Fagin looked at me with interest. "Go on."

Eddie raised an eyebrow at me. I have a habit of coming up with harebrained schemes without informing my husband.

"Yes, Shelly, please tell us your plan."

"Eddie and I will take the firestone from the farm and take it back to the castle where it will be safe," I said.

"Okay, it sounds good," Fagin said. "Let me get the firestone for you." He scaled the barn wall like a squirrel and disappeared into the open loft. A few seconds later, he returned with the very last firestone: a brilliant silver gem gleaming in the barn's lights. He carelessly tossed it towards us, but Eddie caught it and put it into his backpack.

"What is the next part of your plan?" the brownie asked.

I hadn't thought the next part through. "Uh-uh-uh," I said as my brain madly scrambled together a not well thought out plan. I glanced at the tractor. "Does that work?"

"It hasn't been turned on in years," Fagin said.

"That's not a problem," I said. "Eddie can hotwire it."

"I can?" my husband asked.

"Fagin and I can make some Molotov cocktails. We all climb aboard the tractor, and Eddie will break down the barn door with the tractor. As we race through the cornfield, we'll light up our cocktails and burn those creepy scarecrows to the ground!"

Eddie leaned in close to me. "Babe, can I give you some constructive criticism about your plan?" he asked me in a low whisper. "Telepathically."

Sure, honey, I said.

I've never driven a tractor before, much less hotwired one. They aren't exactly the fastest things on earth.

Eddie, you build cars and motorcycles from scratch. You can do this.

Okay, I'll give it a shot. The vampire walked to the large tractor and popped the hood to get familiar with the engine. Then he climbed into the cab and went to work.

While Eddie worked on the tractor, Fagin and I started to gather the Molotov cocktails' materials. The back wall of the barn had a three-tiered shelf filled with empty beer bottles. Apparently, Farmer Swenson loved his moonshine. I grabbed six of them and looked around for some cloth. I searched the barn's bay but found nothing except for two doors in the back. I opened the first door, and my olfactory senses were hit with the smell of gasoline and diesel. Ooh, I found our flammable liquid. Poking my head back out, I called my husband, "Eddie, do you need gas or diesel for the tractor?"

"Gasoline!" he called back. "Did you find some?"

"Yeah!" I yelled back as I spotted a faded clear blue plastic tote with Rags' written on the front. I opened it up and grabbed eight torn hand towels. "There is an entire room with seven or eight filled gas cans, along with some incendiary devices! How many gallons do you need?"

"Three gallons should be enough!"

I stuffed the rags under one arm and lugged two five-gallon cans to the bay. Eddie jumped down from the cab with a smile on his face. "So, how's the tractor coming along?" I asked.

"I can't believe how easy it is to hotwire a tractor!" Eddie said. He took one of the gas cans and filled up the tank. "It's pretty simple. I just had to unscrew and jump the starter wires."

I began to put together my cocktails. First, I tore off strips of rags and dipped them in the gasoline. Then I threaded the rags into each of the bottlenecks, allowing the rags to stick out a few inches. I instructed the reluctant brownie to hold the rag in place while I carefully poured the bottles' flammable liquid. "Perfect," I said proudly. "Not a drop spilled."

"Yeah, you'd better wash your hands if you don't want your flesh to burn off," Fagin said dryly.

I could smell the gasoline wafting off my hands. The grumpy brownie was right, but he didn't have to be so overdramatic about it. "So, is there a sink where I can wash my hands?"

"In the farmhouse."

"Is it connected to the barn?" I asked hopefully.

Fagin shook his head.

We heard a rumble as the tractor engine sputtered to life. Eddie opened the cab door and jumped down. "Let's get the hell out of Dodge!" he said as he carefully grabbed three of the bottles.

"I can't light the cocktails, or I'll burn my hands," I told as I carried the other three and followed him to the tractor.

The vampire gracefully heaved himself up into the tractor cab without spilling a drop of gasoline. "I have an idea. How's your throwing arm?"

"Decent, I guess," I replied as I jumped up beside him.

"You throw them at the scarecrows. I'll light them up."

"I love a plan that doesn't involve me burning my hands to a crisp." I glanced over my shoulder at the brownie, which was still on the floor. "Are you coming?"

He shrugged. "Sure. Why not? This place was a dump anyway." The brownie took a running leap and was inside the cab with us.

Eddie closed the cab door and shifted the tractor into gear. It violently lurched forward, and I grabbed the Molotov cocktails before they spilled. I looked up to see us hurtling at a clip of twenty-miles-per-hour towards the huge barn door. "Uh, honey?" I asked my husband. "What are you doing?"

He pulled up a lever on his right, and the front-end loader lifted up off the ground. "I'm just going to break the door down."

"What!"

"Don't worry, babe! I've got this." With that confident response, my husband pushed the same lever, bringing the frontend loader crashing down onto the barn doors. The wood splintered in two with a loud CRACK!

I happened to glance over to my right and saw a small, black box mounted on the wall. I face-palmed and let out a sigh.

Eddie looked at me. "What?"

"There is a garage door opener on that wall. You could've used that."

"But there is no remote."

I pointed to the little remote control clipped to the sun visor above my husband.

"Okay, but the batteries could be dead," Eddie protested.

I raised an eyebrow at him, but I couldn't hide my smile. I knew he hadn't checked the batteries. He was my sexy vampire who loved the idea of breaking down doors with a tractor.

A shadowy figure jumped onto the back of the cab. A raked hand smashed the back window. Shards of glass flew at us. I immediately hit the floor. "Eddie!" I screamed as a massive piece of the window flew toward the back of his neck.

He turned into mist just before the glass flew through him and into the windshield. The windshield cracked and splintered like a spider web. He changed back and let me know that he was okay.

"That's it!" I shouted angrily. I picked one of the Molotov

cocktails and motioned for my husband to light it up. Once it was

lit, I threw it hard at the scarecrow's chest.

The evil left the scarecrow's eyes and was soon replaced

by a mixture of fear and absolute horror. It didn't have time to

react because I grabbed the window frame with both hands. I

pushed up and swung out with my vampire strength. I knocked

the flaming scarecrow off the tractor. "I am the queen of

Peregrin, and nobody tries to kill my Guardian!"

The scarecrow erupted into flames. Pieces of flaming

straw flew everywhere, igniting everything they touched. I had no

idea the neon corn would be that flammable.

The brownie looked at me in surprise. "You're the new

queen?"

"Yeah," I said as I picked up another cocktail and leaned

out the broken window to light it up on one of the flaming corn

stalks. "Sorry about that."

"Scarecrow at three o'clock!" Eddie shouted.

Once the homemade bomb was on fire, I chucked it at the

leaping scarecrow. Two down, five more to go. "Team

scarecrows: Zero, Team royals: Two!" I shouted at the burning strawman.

"Why didn't you tell me you were the new queen?" Fagin demanded.

"You never asked," I said.

A third scarecrow had jumped on the back of the tractor, and I was about to kick it off when Fagin casually snapped his fingers. One of the scarecrow's overall legs began to unravel. The cloth snagged in the gears of the columbine, and the creature toppled backward. It let out a horrifying scream as the blades ripped it to shreds.

I began to get dizzy as my vision started to blur. I grabbed the back of Eddie's seat to steady myself as I started to blackout. Not another one!

Fagin sits with a young Welkie who is staring at the firestone. "You know, Swenson. This stone will be of great use to us."

"I don't know, Fagin," says Swenson. "Playing with black magic by use of the power of a firestone could be dangerous."

The brownie smiles. "Look at this way. The firestone was placed here for a reason. No more competing for the best crop to deliver to the Demon King. Harness its power to have the greatest crop here in Peregrin!"

"But what if someone tries to steal it from us?"

"Build a dome around the crop and place guards."

"We can't afford guards."

"Who said anything about hiring? I will build guards. Scarecrows that eat anyone who trespasses."

Swenson smiles, no doubt thinking about the riches this firestone would bring to him. "Let's do it."

The scene quickly changes. Swenson is pacing back and forth nervously. "Fagin, this was a bad idea. The scarecrows killed those kids."

The brownie shrugs apathetically. "They shouldn't have been trespassing."

"No one was supposed to get hurt."

"What part of cannibalistic scarecrows don't you get? Accidents will happen."

"You shouldn't have created those things!"

Fagin snaps his fingers, and the barn doors fly open. One of the scarecrows rushes in and grabs the Welkie. The creature begins to tear apart Swenson, with Fagin looking on in disinterest.

"You traitor!" Swenson screams in between agonizing cries of pain. "You will pay. I invoke the Schwitzgebel spell!" A scarecrow decapitates him with a clawed hand.

I came out of the vision with a start. I managed to keep a straight face as I glanced at the brownie. I tapped Eddie on the shoulder.

"What is it?" he asked.

What is a Schwitzgebel spell? I asked telepathically.

It's a spell, which confines a person to a particular space. Only the Welkie can retract the magic unless he is dead, and then a third party can do it.

What does the third party have to do to break the spell?

Not much. They have to get the subject away from the perimeter. Eddie turned and looked at me. *Why do you ask?*

I think I invited a psychopathic, murdering brownie to escape with us.

What?

I glanced at Fagin, who had an evil smile on his face. *I'll explain later, if we make it out alive,* I replied. I gripped Eddie's shoulder as a feeling of dread overcame me.

I was right. The next few minutes happened so fast I didn't have any time to react. "Thank you for all you've done, your Majesties," the brownie said. "Maybe next time I won't kill you!" Then he clapped his hands together, and the tractor exploded.

Eddie and I were thrown off into a cluster of flaming corn stalks. My husband conjured up a green force field ball to protect us from flying tractor parts and pieces of Molotov cocktails. "You okay?" Eddie asked me.

"Yeah, you?" I asked. I looked around at the corn maze, which was engulfed in flames. I came to a horrible realization. There were smoke and fire in an enclosed building. Vampires couldn't die from smoke inhalation, but I didn't want to be hacking all day long. Fortunately, I had an idea. "Two questions. How long can you maintain this force field? Did you ever have any gerbils growing up?"

"Ten minutes at the most. No, I didn't."

I got into a running stance. "Try not to throw up." Then I began to run.

"What are you doing?" Eddie asked as he began to spin around in the force field.

"Getting us out of here! Just maintain the force field!" Using all my vampiric speed, I sent us barreling through the radioactive cornfield. Neon green stalks were flattened underneath us.

Eddie managed to keep his balance and began to run along beside me, doubling the speed. "This is an awesome plan, but don't forget about the glass dome," he said.

"Oh, I haven't." I looked up to see the glass semi-circle rising before us. "Hang on, honey. This might hurt." We broke through the glass with a loud crash and continued to roll until we crashed into a tree. The force field shattered harmlessly around us as Eddie collapsed onto an exhausted heap.

Black shards of glass sparkled in the moonlight as the dome fell apart. It was eerily beautiful and definitely not safe. I took the Tomlinson umbrella from my husband's backpack, wrapped my arm around his waist, and transported us back to the *Monte Carlo*.

Gunther and Cassius met us on the bridge. "Is his Majesty all right?" the satyr asked.

"I'm okay, just exhausted from using a spell too long," Eddie said as I helped him into a chair.

I gave my husband a kiss. "You did good, honey." I turned to the others. "I've got good news and bad news."

Cassius and Gunther looked at me with worry.

I reached into Eddie's backpack. "The good news is we got the firestone." I showed them the silver gem. "The bad news is we accidentally set a murderous brownie on the world."

"Is this brownie's name Fagin?" the airship captain asked.

"Yes," I said. "How did you know?"

"Fagin is a known psychopath who will kill without remorse," Gunther explained.

"Yeah, that became pretty clear when he made the tractor explode," I said. The confused looks on Gunther and Cassius's faces had Eddie and I tell our adventure in the cornfield. Cassius turned the airship towards Mount Hottah as Eddie and I got some much-needed rest. We were going to need it for the final part of my plan.

Chapter Thirteen:
A Sucker is Born

Eddie and I arrived at the mountain home of the pamola. The hurricane-force winds nearly knocked us off the edge of the cliff as we braved our way to the mouth of the cave. "Ready?" Eddie whispered to me.

"I guess so," I said.

"I'm right here beside you if anything goes wrong." Eddie drew me close.

"I know. I just have never done anything like this before." My nerves were shot. This was the first and hopefully last con I would ever pull. At least, my husband's presence lowered my anxiety a little bit.

We walked into the entrance where Laban was sitting on his tacky throne like an impatient child. He looked up to see us.

"Where is it?" he demanded.

"Right here," Eddie said. He dug the firestone out of his backpack and tossed it to Laban.

"You have your firestones, and you must free Hiram," I told him.

Laban laughed as his eyes filled with hunger and power. "You foolish terrestrials," he said as he waved his hand at us. "I had no intention of ever freeing my brother. You handed over your precious firestones without a fight, and now there is no escape. I will rule every possible realm, and no one can stop me!"

Instantly, Eddie and I were encased in the same stasis field with the injured Hiram. I crouched next to the prime minister and let him know everything was going to be okay.

"No, you've endangered the entire queendom," Hiram hissed through the pain.

"Trust me, Mr. Prime Minister," I told him.

Eddie conjured up a ball of energy and threw it at the impenetrable cage. It ricocheted back and forth, and we used our shields for protection. I pulled out Knowledge and sliced through the ball of energy as if it were air. Eddie's jaw dropped in surprise. *Did you know your sword could do that?* He asked me telepathically.

I know it can deflect magic, but not cut through energy, I replied, just as surprised as he was.

Fortunately, doofus over there didn't see your cool trick.

Eddie was right. Once the pamola had the seventh firestone in his hands, he closed his eyes and began to chant something unintelligible. Black, inky wisps of magical energy snaked up from his hands as the firestone started to levitate and spin in mid-air. Soon, the other six gemstones joined in as a bone-chilling coldness filled the room. Eyes still closed, Laban slowly brought the firestones closer and closer together as if he were trying to meld them into one colossal firestone.

I don't know what he was expecting, but it certainly wasn't the clunking sounds of a bunch of rocks hitting together. He opened his eyes and screamed as the gems fell to the ground. The temperature dropped faster and faster as an icy frost covered the room. "What have you done?" he thundered at me.

Even though my teeth were chattering, I stood my ground.

"You got what you wanted."

"I wanted the firestones, not these imitations!" Opening a hole in the stasis field, Laban levitated the rocks at the cage and flung them at us.

I swung Knowledge and sliced through each rock with ease. "Actually, you never specified which firestones you wanted, and those are firestones," I pointed out.

He roared with rage, as he knew he had been played by a "foolish terrestrial." "Where are the real firestones?" he snarled.

"Safe," I replied.

"I will destroy you, you insignificant speck of dust!"

"I don't think so," I said calmly. "You've already broken your promise by not freeing Hiram. A pamola's promise ensures his place here in this realm, doesn't it?"

Laban staggered back as if he had been hit. "No, I will never leave this realm. It belongs to me."

"Not this time," I said. "Peregrin is under my protection, and I'm about to give my first royal decree. By my order, Queen Michelle, ruler of Peregrin, you, Laban the pamola, are banished from this realm for all eternity!" I shouted, with all the authority I could muster.

"No!" Laban screamed as a blinding light appeared out of nowhere, and invisible hands began to pull him into it. Seconds later, he was gone along with the stasis field and heading towards the light.

Eddie knelt beside Hiram and checked his pulse. "Shell, we need to get him some medical attention now! He barely has a pulse." The earth began to shake beneath our feet. Crap! I didn't foresee a cave-in. A piece of the ceiling crashed next to us. My husband picked up the unconscious prime minister in a fireman's carry. "Go! Go!" he shouted to me as the cave started to crumble around us. We raced back to the mouth of the cave as it collapsed behind us. We barely made it out before the mouth crumbled in on itself.

The hurricane winds greeted us and almost pushed us back into the cave-in. I pulled out the Tomlinson from Eddie's backpack and wrapped one arm around the vampire's waist. "Foo mickins *Monte Carlo*." Instantly, all three of us were teleported to the safety of the airship.

A few days later, Eddie and I visited Hiram, recovering in the hospital in a private room. My husband waited outside the room. The pantax formula had worked and was slowly healing his broken and bruised body. He was awake when I came in.

"Forgive me if I do not bow, your Majesty," he said weakly.

"Don't worry, Mr. Prime Minister," I said.

Hiram smiled as he managed to sit up. "How did you fool my brother?"

I smiled. "We had a little help from Gunther Hornicus."

"Gunther Hornicus?"

I nodded.

"He's a good man." Hiram reached for a glass of water on a nearby table. He took a long sip before continuing.

"You're probably wondering what happened to me. May I tell you?"

"Yes, that'd be nice," I answered.

Hiram grunted in pain. He wasn't fully healed. "I was bringing the firestones back from the star where they are refurbished every five hundred years. Laban attacked me and demanded I give him the firestones."

I remembered the power-hungry look in Laban's eyes. "Is ultimate power like a drug to your people?" I asked.

"It is and can destroy entire realms. I managed to escape with major injuries. I knew Laban was hunting me, and I hid the firestones, making it impossible for any pamola to retrieve them."

I wanted to patch things up with the former prime minister. "I know what happened between my grandmother and you."

"Queen Melissa refused to listen to me! I told her not to believe the rumors and use diplomacy instead of an attack. But she acted like a typical royal, and because of that, the Demon Wars devastated our country!" He was almost shouting.

"You're absolutely right," I said. "From what I understand, my grandmother acted without considering the consequences of her actions. She led Peregrin into war."

Hiram gave me a skeptical look. He certainly didn't believe me. I couldn't blame him. After all, my family had betrayed him. The pamola took another sip of his water.

"I know my family has hurt you, and I am sorry. I would like to reinstate you as prime minister."

"Why?" he asked.

"I've heard good things about you, and my husband and I can't run this country on our own. We need your wisdom and your advice."

Hiram wasn't ready to commit, and so he changed the subject. "The firestones are safely locked away?"

"Yes."

"Good, that's where they should be."

"I have some ideas on what to do with them."

Hiram looked shocked, as if I wanted them destroyed. "What?" he demanded.

I put up my hands. "I want to put them to good use. Each firestone is worth 100 trillion dollars. They shouldn't be sitting in a dusty vault. The money from one alone could bring about a public library, an art museum, a zoo, an aquarium, and a sports arena. We create jobs by investing in road repair and hiring a new sheriff's department. These are just a few things which could really get Peregrin back on her feet."

The pamola was silent for a few moments. "You have promise and spunk. I admire that about you."

"Thank you."

"I'll accept your offer, but it will be probationary. If in six months your rule is not within my satisfaction, I will resign permanently."

"Sounds fair." I gave Hiram a firm handshake.

"I would like to ask your Guardian some questions."

Eddie stepped into the room and sat down beside me. He took my hand. "Mr. Prime Minister, what is it that you want to know?" he asked the pamola.

"Why did you become a Guardian?"

"I sort of fell into it. When Shelly and I first met, I had no idea she was royalty."

"Yeah," I said. "We both found out about my heritage a month ago."

Hiram looked surprised but said nothing about it. "What qualifies you to be her Guardian?" he asked.

"I could talk about my experiences as a spy and a bounty hunter. I have one thing that qualifies me: unwavering devotion to Shelly. Not because she's the queen, but because I love her, and I'll protect her with my life."

"Aww, Eddie," I said as I gave him a kiss.

"That's good enough for me," Hiram said, "but you'll still have to go through the training with Master Joab."

"Piece of cake," my husband said confidently.

We got up to leave. "The next cabinet meeting will be in two weeks, Mr. Prime Minister," I told the pamola. "I'll see you there."

COMING SOON

Rescue of the Undead

My Life Among the Undead:

Book 10

By
Camara M. Bragdon

Join the vampire queen and king of Peregrin, Shelly and Eddie Van Helsing, in a spine-chilling adventure as they unravel the mystery of Shelly's missing parents and a string of abductions across Zephyr and beyond. The plot thickens as even their trusted secretary, Gunther Hornicus, goes rogue and disappears. Can they crack the case, unearth Gunther's secret, and save the day? Get ready for a blood-curdling ride!

ABOUT THE AUTHOR

Camara M. Bragdon has since escaped the snowy tundra of Maine and now lives in sunny southwest Florida with her cat. Mistoffelees. When she is not writing, she brings joy and learning as a children's and teen librarian, taking pictures and telling terrible puns. This is her ninth book in the *My Life Among the Undead* series, Visit her website at http://camarambragdonauthor.com